Reviews

Any of David Dorris's books that involve Stunning Steven Edwards or the West Side Kids dives deep into classic movies like the Bowery Boys, Martin and Lewis, Abbot & Costello, and even Kenan & Kel - but updates them with modern humor and adventure. One minute the heroes are playing word games and making me smile, and the next minute they are dashing through bullets, time machines, and maniacal madmen! A great adventure for young readers and readers young at heart!

I was honored to receive an advance reading of this book. And thrilled to know that Davenport, Iowa is well protected by this group of daring do-gooders- Some bumbling and some brave- but all are the finest "detectives" that the Quad Cities will ever know! Not too shabby for this small part of Iowa!

Christopher Murphy
Burlington By the Book
301 Jefferson Downtown Burlington Iowa-52601

Comedy, crime, drama, laughter, confusion, shenanigans, hypnosis, wrestling with a bit of boxing, this book has it all! I like the way the previous books are woven throughout, and that it brings back all of his characters and adds a few new ones. My favorite character is Scooter – he is chaotic, refreshingly naïve and always the hero! And David weaves all of his one liners throughout – try to catch them all!

Robin Rollins
CEO
KOEHLER ELECTRIC

WHAT. THE....TWIST?! This amazing tale of twisted enjoyment based in the wonderful Quad Cities will take you on a journey that is jam-packed with adventure. The spontaneous peaks and valleys of this storyline lead us towards a genuine truth. Or does it?!

How can we, as readers, fully express that...WE WANT MORE!! It cannot end here?! I do NOT think he's down for the count...just yet. It's Rally Time, folks!!

Jessica Hoeksema
Quad City Resident
Patient Advocate Specialist through our local area Health Care System

A cast of characters brings Stunning Stephen Edwards, a detective as well as a talented boxer, into their effort to catch a villain and stop a crime. This story involves several characters with various crime-solving skills and how they each help Stephen catch Dr. Zodiac. Enjoy how the group solves the crime together!

Suzy VenHorst
Bettendorf, Iowa

I just finish reading Wrestling with Death! Once I started it, I couldn't put it down! There are so many twists in it! I needed to find out "who dunnit"! The details of every character come alive as if they are real people. Very interesting read. Filled with mystery and comedy! Very easy to read at any age.

Carrie Quinn
Office Assistant
Lynch Heating & Plumbing

About the Book Rack

The basic operation of the store has always been to accept books in trade for store credit and allow customers to use that credit toward the purchase of a different used paperback book. It is an elegantly simple process that gives significant benefit to the avid reader while allowing The Book Rack to thrive.

Owned by Bob & Claudia Applegate, the inventory of The Book Rack has to over 65,000 today. The inventory is very dynamic adding titles with each trade and reducing with each sale.

Bob Applegate
The Book Rack
Davenport, Iowa - 563-355-2310
cell - 309-738-0662
Like us on Facebook: http://www.facebook.com/QCBookRack
http://thebookrackqc.com/

Live Life Your Way

Life is too short and happiness is so rare.

Knowing yourself is the beginning of all wisdom. Living a life avoiding doing something stupid does only one thing for you. It never gives you the opportunity to see what you really can do. You need to chose honesty over perfection every time, then have the ability to adapt and overcome. Failure will only build your character.

If you've got nothing going for you today, you need to get yourself together. Now is the time to make up your mind, because you want to make sure all the good times aren't slipping away. Smile, grow, want, crave, feel, always make every minute count.

Some days you have to rise above the storm and you will find the sunshine. Sometimes we need fantasy to survive the reality. Be silly. Be fun. Every time you find some humor in a difficult situation, create your own sunshine.

One of the best lessons you can learn in life is trying to master how to remain calm. To do that, make your own kind of music. Remember, a smile is king and then to begin to sing even if nobody sings along with you. Be different. Be you, because life is too short to be anything but happy, and you will win.

The happiest people don't have the best of everything. They just make the best of everything they have.

You can never go wrong by giving a person an even brake and always play fair and square with others by helping them when they need us. We need to treat people with respect and give them the dignity they deserve.

It's your life. Don't ever let anyone make you feel guilty for living life your way.

David W. Dorris

Wrestling with Death

Fourth Book Of The Series

Comedy, Crime, Drama, With Stunning Stephen Edwards As Detective Stunning Stephen Edwards In

DAVID W. DORRIS

authorHOUSE

AuthorHouse™
1663 Liberty Drive
Bloomington, IN 47403
www.authorhouse.com
Phone: 833-262-8899

Published by AuthorHouse 05/14/2021

ISBN: 978-1-6655-2626-5 (sc)
ISBN: 978-1-6655-2627-2 (hc)
ISBN: 978-1-6655-2625-8 (e)

CONTENTS

Chapter One
WHO IS DR. FINE

The date is now October 1st 2018. The headlines in the newspaper in Davenport, Iowa reads, "No New Word Of Pro Wrestler Found Dead On Roof Of Hotel". Other stories in the newspaper are, "World Middle Weight Boxing Champion, Stunning Stephen Edwards Returns to Davenport", "Jerry Dickerson And His Associates Are Released From Prison" and "Dr. Preston Fine Has New Book Published Called The Healthy Benefits Of Hypnotism".

It is now 10:00 a. m.. Rex Tarillo and T. J. Columbo are sitting in Rex's office at The Davenport Police Station talking about Jerry Dickerson and his crew being released from prison a week ago and going to The Moline Airport tomorrow to pick up Stephen Edwards at 3:00 p. m., when Rex's wife Margret Tarillo enters her husband's office with the morning newspaper.

"Hello Columbo", greeted Margret. "Rex, I've got to show you something in the news paper. Dr. Preston Fine has written a new book called, "The Healthy Benefits Of Hypnotism". This book of his makes some good reading. Dr. Fine is giving a demonstration at 7:00 p. m. tomorrow evening to the news media at his office in downtown Davenport on East 3rd Street. For $500.00 he would hypnotize me if I can make an appointment. Would you take me?

You know that I have never been mentally the same since I had to deal with the events that occurred after you became "The Small Fry."

It is really getting to me. The strain is more than I can handle. I haven't been able to sleep very well and when I do, I have awful nightmares.

Nobody has been able to help me. You would think that somebody would know how to help me. I don't know who else to turn to for help. I want to see if Dr. Preston Fine can help me."

"I know Margret. I know," answered Rex. "I am very worried about your health. You and me went through a lot the day Scooter came as a chemistry student with The West Side Kids, to The University of Davenport and enrolled in my class. If it wasn't for Scooter mixing up his chemicals with mine that I created to drink, to keep me from loosing my temper, none of this would have happened. I drank his chemicals by mistake and became a forty inch small fry. It all was a nightmare with Scooter. Scooter is like the interest on a mortgage. He's hard to escape."

"Rex, that may have been a nightmare," replied Columbo. "So Scooter does stupid things like when he switched the chemicals that made you a small fry. Then he made a bomb in your class and threw it out the window where it landed on your new car, blowing it up. After that you took him over to The Dean's Office with Hannibal, while in the Dean's Office, Scooter struck again braking The Dean's expensive statue twice.

A lot of good also happened after you was restored to you original size Detective Sgt. Tarrilo. You not only became a great Detective and my partner, you also married a beautiful woman who stands by you through thick and thin. I'm sure even when you was that small fry, Margret made you feel ten feet tall.

Now that your friends with Scooter, Hannibal and The West Side Kids, you and I work with their Detective Agency on some of our cases. You can't help but like Scooter now that you understand him."

"I know. Scooter really does have a good heart and he means well," answered Rex. "He is really harmless. Since I understand Scooter, I guess I have joined the rest of you in trying to keep Scooter out of trouble. Sometimes it can be a hard thing to do, because you never know what he's going to do next.

I really think we should take Margret to meet Dr. Fine. She is under a very great emotional strain. Dr. Fine may be the one to help her," insisted Rex.

"Oh, that is wonderful. It looks like I'm finally going to get some help," replied an excited Margret.

"Just to see how good he really is, I think we should invite Scooter to go with us," added Rex. "If Dr. Fine doesn't go bananas first, he may even help Scooter."

"What a mean trick? What a mean trick to pull on Dr. Fine, using Scooter to test Dr. Fine?" yelled Margret. "Nobody can help Scooter, nobody. I want to see if Dr. Fine can help me, not Scooter. If we take Scooter with us, Dr. Fine will never want to help me."

"Calm down, Margret," insisted Rex. "I want to see if this Dr. Fine is on the level. If this Dr. Fine decides to help you, I want to make sure your getting the right kind of help. Trust me Margret. I think if Scooter goes with us, we will get a lot of our questions answered."

"Dr. Fine's phone number is listed here in the newspaper. Can I give Dr. Fine a call right now?" asked Margret as Hannibal and Scooter entered Rex's Office.

"Sure Margret. If Dr. Fine can make you feel better, give him a call," replied Rex.

"Is there something wrong with Margret?" asked Hannibal. "Maybe there is something we can do to help."

"Hey fellows, doesn't Margret look pretty today?" asked Scooter. "Margret, how would you like me to make you some French Scrambled Eggs?"

Looking right in Scooter's eyes, Hannibal scolded Scooter by saying, "Stop it Scooter. There is no such thing as French Scrambled Eggs and you know it. I've heard of French Fries and French Toast, but I have never heard of French Scrambled Eggs. Scooter, you are laboring under a delusion. What are you trying to do, kid all of us?"

"I don't care what you say. I can make them. All I need is to get some eggs from a French Chicken," explained Scooter. "That's how you make French Toast is with eggs from a French Chicken."

"Just who is this Dr. Fine?" asked Hannibal.

"Dr. Preston Fine is the one who wrote the best selling book everyone is talking about, The Healthy Benefits of Hypnotism," answered Margret.

"Oh, yeah. I know who that Dr. Fine is that wrote that book. A lot of people don't approve of what he does and they say that just because he wears that silly mustache, the book is a big joke," noted Hannibal. "Let me get this straight. You mean you want Dr. Hocus Pocus, the scam artist to do a con job on you by hypnotizing you?"

"For $500.00 he won't just hypnotize me. He will regress me back in time before Rex drank Scooter's chemicals and became The Small Fry," insisted Margret.

"$500.00, that's a mighty fine price that Dr. Fine charges," laughed Scooter. "Get it. mighty fine price. Dr. Fine, oh never mind. My Aunt Clara belle was regressed back in time to when she found out that she was Cleopatra. Now she has my Uncle George building her a pyramid in the back yard. Come on, laugh, will you?"

"Yes Scooter, That was funny, ha, ha, ha," laughed Uncle Columbo.

"5.00.00 ain't chicken feed. I know how to get Margret to relax all of the time and I can save her the $500.00," insisted Scooter.

"Funny boy, just how can you do that for Margret?" inquired Hannibal.

"I'll tell you how," Scooter went on to say. "First you get some rain water from Florida. Then you put two drops of Florida rain water in a glass and fill the rest of the glass with whiskey. Then you drink it. Do that several times a day and you will never have a care or a worry."

"Let me illuminate you. Save your money," insisted Hannibal. "This sounds like an illegal plot to me. Dr. Fine is a fake. I've heard of this nut. Dr. Fine would go to the zoo and spend hours there. He believes animals can talk to him and each other. He just imagines all of this."

"What do they say?" asked Scooter.

"Shut up," snarled Hannibal.

"That's not a very nice thing to say," replied Scooter. "That reminds me. Do you know what an investigator is?"

"Scooter, you should know that one," Hannibal fired back. "He's a Detective."

"Actually an investigator is alligator with a vest on," replied Scooter.

"Scooter, you just do not stop," laughed Uncle Columbo. "You are really one of a kind."

"I saw Dr. Fine's picture in his book," Margret went on to say. "He is very handsome and has the face of a saint."

"A Saint Bernard," laughed Hannibal.

"If everything you say about this Dr. Fine is true, we need to expose him as a phony," Rex replied to everyone.

"How do we do that?" inquired Hannibal.

"Hello, is this information?" asked Scooter talking into his phone. "Is Dr. Preston Fine a phony?"

"You Dumb Ox. Give me that phone!" yelled Hannibal grabbing it out of Scooter's hand.

"Fellows, would you like to go with us tomorrow to meet Dr. Fine?" inquired Rex.

"Just tell us when and where and we will be there," offered Hannibal.

"Meet us here at the station tomorrow at 6:00 p. m.," instructed Rex. "I want to wait until tomorrow, because Stunning Stephen Edwards will be here to have a meeting with us before we go visit Dr. Fine at 7:00 p. m.."

"Dr. Fine, that name sounds familiar," recalled Scooter. "I can't go to Dr. Fine's Office tomorrow. I have to go to work at the casino tomorrow. Rex, Uncle Columbo, I'm a taxpayer and you work for me. So I order you to go to Dr. Fine's Office without me."

"You can go with us to Dr. Fine's Office," insisted Hannibal. "You haven't worked at the casino for the last six months."

"That explains it," reasoned Scooter.

"Just what does that explain?" boomed Hannibal.

"That's why I haven't been paid every week," exclaimed Scooter. "I still want to remind you that I'm a taxpayer when I'm working."

"If I could find you a job, would you be willing to go back to work?" asked Hannibal.

"Not now. I have to be free to go to Dr. Fine's Office tomorrow," replied Scooter.

"Scooter, What did you mean when you said Dr. Fine's name sounds familiar?" inquired Rex.

"Do you remember when Stephen was working with us as The Invisible Man trying to expose Jerry Dickerson and his gang when they were in a racket paying off boxers to take a fall?" recalled Scooter.

"Ya, I remember. Where does Dr. Fine fit in?" asked Rex.

"Jerry Dickerson's girlfriend, Dixie Doneright took me to her uncle's apartment to find the envelope that Stephen wanted back," Scooter went on to say. "The papers in the envelope told of the dealings of Jerry Dickerson getting the boxing managers to have their boys take a fall. Dixie invited me to sit on the couch next to Dr. Fine. Dr. Fine tried to get information from me about Stephen by hypnotizing me."

"Stephen will be back in town tomorrow," explained Rex. "I'm sure he will want to go with us to meet this local author. Columbo and I are going to pick Stephen up at The Moline Airport at 3:00 p. m. tomorrow. Do you boys want to go with us?"

"Since I don't have to go to work at the casino, I'll go," replied Scooter. "It will be A Fine Day to see Stephen again. He's the squarest, finest wonderful guy and has a lot of dignity. You have to go a long way to find a guy like that. You won't find anybody better."

"Scooter, you do know that Stephen is The World Middle Weight Boxing Champion?" added Columbo.

"When Stephen gets back home, will he be the toughest man in The Quad Cities?" asked Scooter.

"Let's not kid ourselves, Scooter. Stunning Stephen Edwards will be the toughest man in The Quad Cities," explained Columbo. "Stephen is a two fist ed man of action and is not that sort of a person to back away from a fight. He is like a royal flush in a poker game. He's unbeatable.

One of the reasons we asked him to come back to Davenport is to help us as a Detective. Stephen is an enemy who makes him an enemy. He is always on the side of the right and a friend of those who have no friends. He is always helping somebody when when they are being picked on.

Since he is a boxer, maybe he can help us solve the mystery about the dead wrestler found on the roof at the hotel where Jerry Dickerson lives."

"All I know, Stephen is my friend and he will always be my friend," answered Scooter. "If Stephen wants to go to Dr. Fine's Office, then I'm going to skip going to work so I can be there with Stephen."

"We just talked about that. You don't work at the casino anymore. How can you skip going to work?" scolded Hannibal.

"I know I don't work there anymore," insisted Scooter. "That's because I gave up gambling."

"Come on Scooter. That's enough. Let's get back to the office," ordered Hannibal.

Chapter Two

DEAD WRESTLER MEANS TROUBLE FOR JERRY DICKERSON

Jerry Dickerson and his gang has been released from prison for a week. They have now moved back into the same rooms they had at the hotel in downtown east Davenport before they went to prison.

It is now 6:00 p. m., the night that Dr. Fine is going to talk about his new book to the news media. Jerry and his boys, Ace, The Assassin, Mugs, Danny, Lefty and Shorty are sitting in his apartment listening to Jerry talk. The subject at hand is the story in the newspaper concerning about the professional wrestler found dead on the roof of their hotel.

"The story in the newspaper about the wrestler found dead on the roof of this hotel is going to mean trouble for us," explained Jerry to his boys. "We all got out of prison and are on parole. The police are going to be looking at us with suspicious eyes. We may be planning another devious scheme, but it will never involve murder. It looks like we will have to be nosing around to find the culprit who is responsible for this."

"I don't want to go back to the slammer, because it cost me a lot of fresh air," replied Ace."No more schemes for me. I want to be free. I want to box."

"I have a friend that will box you," beamed Lefty.

"And who would that be?" questioned Ace.

"He works for a mortuary here in Davenport," answered Lefty.

"Very funny," roared Ace. "I ought to box your ears off. Then you can tell me how funny that is."

"Ace, Lefty, stop it or I'm going to box the ears off of both of you," demanded Jerry.

"I agree with Ace about not having any more schemes," added Danny. "We need to keep our hands in our pockets and instead of the pockets of somebody else. Let's do something la git."

"My manager kept my gym on Elmore Avenue, by the casino going while we were in prison." Jerry continued to say. "I guess we can run my gym the honest way. If we do, we're going to have to get more boxers to make a go of it. Some of us may even have to go to work."

"You mean we'll really have to go to work?" asked a surprised Danny.

"Yes," answered Jerry. "I may have to find jobs for all of you."

"Does that mean you're going to find a job for yourself and go to work?" asked Mugs.

"Me go to work. Not on your life. I'm the brains of this outfit. Besides, I have to take care of my gym," insisted Jerry.

"Now I want to remind all of you, we were all invited by Michael, The Magnificent, Dr. Fine's manager to go over to our friend, Dr. Fine's Office. He wrote a book called, "The Healthy Benefits Of Hypnotism". Knowing Dr. Fine, its got to be some kind of devious scheme of his own, because he has never put in an honest days work in his life."

"You mean he's like us?" added Danny.

"Yes Danny, he's like us. If it look like a money making racket, I think we should volunteer to be his partners," laughed Jerry. "I hear he is involved with my girl, Dixie Doneright. Now that I'm back in town, I'm going to explain to Preston Fine about the benefits of leaving his hands off of Dixie Doneright. I also want to meet this Michael, The Magnificent that he's hooked up with. Dr. Fine is also going to demonstrate hypnotism. I think we better go. It starts at 7:00 p. m."

Chapter Three
MEETING WITH REX

While Jerry Dickerson is talking to his crew, Stephen, Columbo, Hannibal and Scooter are in Rex's Office for a meeting.

"I want to speak to everyone," Rex began to say. "Columbo and I are in the middle of a murder investigation of a pro wrestler found dead on the roof of the hotel where Jerry Dickerson and his rats live. Columbo and I wrote up a report of what we found out and turned it into the captain.

Columbo and I have some ideas about this case. It's certainly not a cut and dried case. There are too many theories. So far it's been like a dog chasing his tale. We're getting no place fast.

A happy solution in the light is never happy remaining in the dark. Questions have always been what they contain.

Stephen, that is why I asked you to come back to Davenport. Columbo and I would first like to congratulate you as The World Middle Weight Boxing Champion. Since this may involve Jerry Dickerson and his gang, I thought you and The West Side Kids would like to be in on this. To make this official, the captain wants to make you a temporary Police Detective."

"I'm very happy to lend my assistance," answered Stephen. "Here we go again. I wonder what we're in for this time."

"Columbo and I have an idea about this case," explained Rex. "Detective Justin Murphy who you know, is a convicted murderer that was brought to justice by Columbo and me for the most brutal murder. He broke free of his shackles a couple months ago and escaped into the middle of the night.

We have been told that there is a Doctor Miles living in The Quad Cities who specialized in giving new faces to those who want to escape the past. We think that Detective Murphy has a new face and lives at the same hotel as Jerry Dickerson, because he has a score to settle with Jerry.

Crime is always punished. Justice can be brought to this dead wrestler. Justice is like a virtue. It brings its own reward. As one copper to another, the conviction of this most dangerous murderer will bring peaceful sleep to Columbo and me.

It may be a coincidence that Detective Murphy may be hiding behind a new face. To discover who he really is we will need his fingerprints, because fingerprints never lie."

"I always believed that a coincidence is like an ancient egg. It always leaves an unpleasant smell," added Stephen.

"That's right Stephen. We need to locate the bad egg in the picnic basket. Rex and I believe that this suspect is an expert at deceit. After all, that's his business.

A witness saw something between a Dracula and a Zombie roaming the halls of the hotel where Jerry Dickerson lives," added Columbo. "Somebody is hiding behind a mask that resembles a Zombie. This person made it look like blood was dripping from his mouth. He also wore a turbine, with a white sheet over his body. It all looks like its part of a gag.

The police was after this pro wrestler who was murdered. He was going to blab to Rex and me about an illegal wrestling scheme that was going on in the wrestling world."

"I blab a lot and other people blab back," interrupted Scooter. "I don't remember half of what I blab about."

"Oh, I suppose you think that's funny?" scolded Hannibal.

"Well, you have to think about it a while before you get it," answered Scooter.

"Scooter, stop you're blabbing and keep quite. Let Uncle Columbo finish," demanded Hannibal. "I think without your assistance, this case will be solved a lot faster."

"I'm sorry Uncle Columbo. You can continue to blab and tell us what the wrestler was going to blab about. I'm listening," promised Scooter.

"Thanks Scooter for your assistance in letting me continue to blab," laughed Columbo. "As I was saying, we also know that the wrestler called his manager telling him that somebody knew all about him. He asked his manager to protect him and what he should do next. He was told to take the elevator on the seventh floor in the hotel to the lobby. After he got on the elevator, he was killed to hide the truth.

He died from a fall from a great height. Someone wants us to believe he fell seven stories up. It looks like the wrestler had company, because the killer was on friendly terms with the wrestler to get that close to him. We found a note in his hand that read, "Scorpio is the unfortunate symbol of death" and a bloody heel print next to the wrestler. We have to catch this killer now. It's only a matter of time before he strikes again and kills somebody else."

"What do you expect us to do?" asked Stephen.

"Rex and I need all of your help in this murder investigation," answered Columbo.

"Stephen, I want you to go with me to see the captain about officially making you a Detective," instructed Rex. "Dr. Preston Fine wrote a book called, "The Healthy Benefits Of Hypnotism". He is giving a demonstration to the news media at 7:00 p. m.. I want us all to be at that demonstration. After the captain makes you a Detective, I want us all to go to Dr. Fine's demonstration. I always like to be prepared to use the element of surprise. After we visit Dr. Fine, I want to make a surprise visit with Jerry Dickerson."

Chapter Four

DR. FINE, THE HYPNOTIST AND HIS GUESTS

It is now 7:00 p. m. and the members of the news media are standing around a table full of refreshments. Dixie Doneright is standing at the table with the men from the news media offering them more to drink and eat.

"Dixie, I only asked you to help serve the food. Leave the food alone and quit making a pig out of yourself," instructed Dr. Preston Fine.

"What's the matter? Isn't the food any good?" asked Dixie.

"Just do what I told you," replied Dr. Fine.

"Does anybody want some of this stuff?" inquired Dixie. "The food isn't bad."

The telephone rings and Dixie walks over to the desk to answer the phone.

"Joe, help yourself to more ice for your drinks", offered Dr. Fine.

"I need more ice," Joe replied as he watched Dixie walk away. "I know what melted my ice."

Walking up to the table, a man identified himself as Dr. Fine's manager introduced himself to the news media. "I'm Michael, The Magnificent. Would you excuse us gentlemen? Come on Preston. Let's go out on the balcony. I need to talk to you."

Once on the balcony, Michael continued to say, "I want to have a heart to heart talk with you. Dixie Doneright, that blonde assistant of yours. You need to get rid of her. She is distracting our whole operation."

"Is that so. Is that so. That can't be right," replied Dr. Fine. "There is nothing wrong with Dixie and I would do anything for her. Can't you see she has the innocence of a child?"

"How do you mean the innocence of what? Look at the way she walks. She is far from having the innocence of a child," ranted Michael.

"She can't help it," explained Preston. "When she was a child, her mother made her wear tight shoes."

"We have a great racket going for us. If she keeps this up, we'll have to find another racket with a devious scheme," insisted Michael.

"What on earth do you mean? You make me sound like a fake and making my book a fraud," roared Preston. "I'm in charge here. I enjoy using my power over the lives of others and believe I have the power to pass one one person into the body of another."

"You really believe that, don't you? This operation is going to your head. Just because you wrote this book called, "The Healthy Benefits of Hypnotism", it doesn't give you any powers you talk about in your book," snarled Michael. "You and I know it's part of our devious scheme. We have a criminal plot like no other, because it's stranger than the average. The people who read your book really believe you can do these things.

I found you when you were working for Jerry Dickerson and helped you when you needed a friend. You was almost broke before you meant me. After Jerry Dickerson and his misfits went to prison, I helped you write your book and made you famous. It's your job to hypnotize women with money and refer them to me as Dr. Nejino due to their mental health you create.

Jerry Dickerson and his men are out of jail and that great big beautiful blonde is Jerry's girl friend. Jerry is not going to stand for this. I don't want to take any chances of any scandal or black mail. Get rid of her now! We better get back inside."

As Michael The Magnificent and Preston Fine join the news media, Joe yells out, "Dr. Fine, Tell us about your book. We're all looking for more information about your book. We want to hear more about it. We also want you to begin that demonstration we came to see. We need anything that is useful, so we can write our story. I think it's going to be a great story."

From the other side of the room another voice was heard. "Mr. Dr. Preston Fine, who were you before you became a quack?" yelled Stephen.

"Who said that? Who is this man?" yelled Michael The Magnificent. "Come closer, so I can talk to you. I'm Dr. Quack's, I mean to say Dr. Fine's manager, Michael, The Magnificent."

"Since when does a quack need a manager?" replied Stephen as he walked up to Michael. "Are you also a quack?"

"Who let you in? Your not on the guest list," said Michael.

"It's probably an oversight," answered Stephen.

"I consider that the perfect oversight," suggested Michael. "Who are you and what are you horning in for? Who are these people with you?"

"These are my associates. This is Detective Sgt. Rex Tarillo and his wife Margret. Then we have Detective Sgt. T. J. Columbo, Scooter and Hannibal. My name is Detective Stunning Stephen Edwards."

"So you're Stunning Stephen Edwards. I recognized you when you walked through that door. Who invited you to my demonstration?" asked Dr. Fine.

"How did you know who I was?" answered Stephen.

"Who doesn't know the Famous Stunning Stephen Edwards, The World Middle Weight Boxing Champion?"

"Dr. Fine, I wanted to see your demonstration. Look, I brought $500.00 in the hopes you would hypnotize me," requested Margret. "I have been terribly upset lately and have problems sleeping. When I do get to sleep, I have horrible nightmares. After reading your book I have in my hand and after meeting you, I was hoping you could help me."

Looking down at the $500.00, Dr. Fine replied,"Of course, of course dear lady. That's what I'm here for, to help people like you. I like you. You've got spirit. Come over and sit in this chair by my desk."

"Not so fast. How can you stand there and insult our intelligence?" Stephen broke in to say. "Rex, Margret, If you don't mind, I want this genius to hypnotize me first if he can."

"Go ahead and hypnotize Stephen," demanded the reporter. "This is what we all came to see. This will make a great story."

"I invited all of you from the news media here to promote my book. Now all of you will be witness's to what I can do," beamed Dr. Fine. "I have the power and I know I can hypnotize The Great Stunning Stephen Edwards. I will gladly do this for no charge just to demonstrate the benefits of being hypnotized and to shut Stephen up about calling me a quack."

"Go ahead Stephen. Your such a nice boy. You go first," offered Margret. "I don't mind waiting."

"Hannibal, I see what you mean about Dr. Fine getting animals to shut up," recalled Scooter. "If he could get you to shut up, I would give him $500.00."

"Where are you going to get $500.00 to pay Dr. Fine?" asked Hannibal.

"From my next paycheck," answered Scooter.

"I thought we discussed this. You don't have a next paycheck," growled Hannibal.

"Stephen, can I borrow $500.00?" requested Scooter.

"Don't bother Stephen," instructed Hannibal. "He's busy."

"I'm going to sit in this chair here while this genius exposes his intelligence to every one. He'll probably end up hypnotizing himself," exclaimed Stephen. "By the way Scooter, before we get started, can you tell me what time it is?"

"Do I look like a sun dial to you?" asked Scooter.

"Never mind General. Just forget it," replied Stephen. "Will you stand behind my chair. We need to keep an eye on this quack, alias Dr. Fine."

"When you say we, you mean me. Some people don't like being starred at. I have to go. I just want to get out of here," replied an anxious Scooter. "You didn't give me a chance to tell you before, but I think I left the motor running in the car. I have to go. My friend and I are in a bit of a hurry."

"Scooter, what's the matter with you? You didn't drive. Hannibal isn't going anywhere with you right now. Are you nervous?" asked Stephen. "You look very nervous."

"Oh, I don't want to do this because I am a nervous guy," replied Scooter.

"There is nothing to worry about. You are at the safest place in town with Rex, Columbo, Hannibal and me here with you. Your as safe in here as if you were at home taking a bath."

"I hope your right, because I don't like this joint. I would rather be at home taking a bath right now," reasoned Scooter.

"Are you going to help me or can't I trust you?" questioned Stephen.

"No, once and for all, no. I'm not doing it," cried Scooter.

"Come on. Come on. Scooter, knock it off and do what Stephen says," ordered Hannibal. "You watch Dr. Fine and make sure he doesn't try to put anything over on Stephen or I'm going to hypnotize you right in your bath tub. Do you understand me?"

"Oh why not? All right. I'll do it, even though I don't want to," mumbled Scooter. "I'm scared enough as it is, but Dr. Fine won't catch me napping."

"That sounds like my pal," laughed Stephen.

"Before we get started, I need something shinny for you to look at," Dr. Fine went on to say. "Dixie, would you give me one of your ear rings to use for this demonstration?"

"Here poopsie," beamed Dixie as she handed Dr. Fine one of her ear rings.

"Stephen, I want to hypnotize you to get you to think," Dr. Fine began to say.

"Is that going to hurt?" asked Stephen.

"Of course this is not going to hurt," replied Dr. Fine. "Did you really think this was going to hurt?"

"Only when I laugh," insisted Stephen. "I think I can take it. I'm not here to think. Just get on with it. Go ahead and hypnotize me if you can."

"OK, let's begin. Keep your eyes open and your mouth shut. Be relaxed, completely relaxed. Look at this shiny ear ring go back and forth, back and fourth," requested Dr. Fine.

"You want me to keep both of my eyes open?" asked Stephen.

"You have to keep both of them open. Now pay attention to what I'm telling you. Will you just relax and concentrate?" protested Dr. Fine. "I want complete concentration."

Stephen then began a steady twitch in the right shoulder, right arm and eye.

"Dr. Fine, do you think I'm twitching," asked Stephen.

"Obviously you are twitching," observed Dr. Fine.

"Well I'm not twitching," answered Stephen.

"Your not twitching," replied Dr. Fine.

"He's not twitching," Dr. Fine went on to say.

"That's enough of this nonsense. That was a very funny act you put on. You must think you're pretty cute." growled Dixie Doneright as she was holding a 2 liter bottle of cola in one hand and an empty paper glass in the other. "The decent people in this town shouldn't be bothered by the likes of you. You should be locked up."

"Are you talking to me?" asked Stephen with a surprised look on his face.

"Yes, I'm talking to you," answered Dixie. "Because your not cooperating and doing what Dr. Fine says, you need to pay him his $500.00 fee for trying to hypnotize you."

"Don't get excited. Don't get excited," promised Stephen. "I'm sorry if I upset you."

"Well come on! Pay up and don't try anything funny!" ordered Dixie.

"I wouldn't let her get irritated. Women always get mad when you laugh at them. She's a spunky little thing. You better do what she says," reasoned Hannibal. "She's smart enough and pretty enough to make you do it."

"She is kind of easy to look at. I guess I better sit here and stay relaxed," answered Stephen. "Since I have to pay you, go ahead and get the money out of the left pocket of my shirt. Let me hold your paper cup and your bottle of cola while you do that."

Dixie then began to hand Stephen the paper glass and the bottle of cola as Stephen reached for them. In a flash, Dixie decided to hold on to the paper glass and bottle of cola and exclaimed as she was trying to pour the cola into her glass, "Oh no you don't! Keep your ole money, it's probably stolen anyway and quit trying to make a monkey out of Dr. Fine!"

"Then tell Dr. Fine to give me back my banana and then I will cooperate," answered Stephen. "By the way, you need to unscrew the cap and take it off the bottle to get the cola out."

"Oh you, you trouble maker!" exclaimed Dixie.

"Dixie, settle down so we can start again," instructed Dr. Fine.

Looking over at Scooter, Hannibal boomed, "Scooter, stop that twitching and watch Dr. Fine."

"I'm watching. I'm watching," replied a nervous Scooter.

"All right, let's start again," instructed Dr. Fine. "Relax and concentrate. If you cooperate, maybe I can help you with some of your problems."

"Oh, are you a philosopher?" asked Stephen.

"That's immaterial to me. You have nothing to say about this. You know what I mean. You must be completely relaxed," insisted Dr. Fine. "Don't talk any more."

"Why?" asked Stephen.

"I must insist on complete concentration," pleaded Dr. Fine. "You keep opening your mouth and now your starting to aggravate me."

"All right, I'm relaxed and concentrating," promised Stephen. "Remember Scooter, complete concentration."

"Now watch closely and look at this ear ring as it swings back and forth, back and forth, back and forth," instructed Dr. Fine as he held Dixie's ear ring in front of Stephen's eyes again. "Relax your entire body, your neck, your shoulders, your arms. Your getting tired, very tired. Close your eyes. Now your getting sleepy, very sleepy."

"I am? I mean I am," replied Stephen.

"Now your under my power. You will sleep deeper and deeper," Dr. Fine continued to say. "You will hear only my voice. You will listen to me, only me.

Now tell me the truth. Do you have unusual dreams? Do you have dreams, dreams of people trying to kill you?" asked Dr. Fine.

"Now that you mention it, That's a very interesting thing that you're asking me. I do have a dream that keeps haunting me," replied Stephen.

"Now we're getting someplace. What do you see in these dreams?" asked Dr. Fine.

"I dream of squirrels, everywhere. The squirrels pop up before me all the time. All they do is ask me questions and they drive me mad, mad, mad, because all they talk about is nuts."

"Stephen, how can I prove to you that I'm not a quack if you won't relax and concentrate so I can hypnotize you?" asked Dr. Fine. "Now let's start over and be relaxed so you can begin to sleep, sleep, sleep. Begin to sleep deeper, deeper, deeper. You will do everything I tell you to do. Your a bird and your going to flap your wings."

"See what I told you Scooter," explained Hannibal. "This nut wants Stephen to be a bird so he can talk to him. Did you hear me Scooter?"

"What a lot of phony junk," laughed Stephen. "I knew it. I knew he was a phony. Are we going to let him get away with that?"

"Now I think I have my story to write about Dr. Fine," said Richard who was from the news media.

"Stephen, did you stage this whole thing?" asked Rex.

"I sure did Rex. You catch on fast. Scooter, was you standing there watching Dr. Fine like I asked you to do?" questioned Stephen. "Dr. Fine is a fraud. Scooter, did you hear me? This is no time to be sleeping or standing there watching the world go by. Say, there is something funny about this."

"OK, so I didn't hypnotize Stephen. If every body in the news media will give me another chance, I can still give you that story to promote my book, The Healthy Benefits of Hypnotism." admitted Dr. Fine. "It looks like I hypnotized Stephen's friend. If there are no objections, I'll continue with this boy. Stephen, would you get up from that chair so we can help your friend to the chair? Before we start, I need to know you're friends name."

"You don't know what your in for. It's not going to be as easy as you think. Don't you realize what you have done?" laughed Hannibal. "His name is Scooter."

"It's not as bad as all that. I know what I'm doing," explained Dr. Fine.

"This should be an unusual experiment for you. It's going to take somebody smarter than you to get the best of Scooter. This ought to be good," teased Hannibal. "After Scooter is hypnotized, then his sub conscience will try and speak. It will be like his cell phone is out of order. Even a clarinet will not speak when it's stomach is empty. Then when he does start to speak, he won't be able to stop, because he isn't equipped with a self stopper."

"Dr. Fine, I should be sitting in that chair getting hypnotized by you, not this, this imbecile," cried Margret. "He's the reason I came to get your help. Rex, talk to Dr. Fine. Tell him how bad I need his help."

"Now, now Margret, calm down. Please be patient," replied Rex. "I want to see this. Think about it Margret. This our chance to even things out with Scooter."

"Nothing better happen to my friend. Don't try any tricks, Mr. Fine. Because if something goes wrong, I'm going to break every bone in your body," promised Stephen.

"Stephen, calm down. Between you and Margret, your going to blow a gas cut. Stephen, I don't know about you, but Margret has a slight speech impediment. Every now and then she stops talking so she can breath. Even when Margret is happy, as a Police Detective, I cannot fathom the depth of a woman's smile. Columbo and I will be watching Dr. Fine," Rex continued to say. "Dr. Fine better be who he says he is and take proper care of Scooter or else he will have to deal with the law. Any questions?"

"I'm sorry Rex. I guess I'm just over protective of my little buddy," insisted Stephen. "There is nothing I wouldn't do for him."

"Stephen, two things are going to happen," reasoned Hannibal. "If anything, this quack, this idiot that calls himself a hypnotist can only improve how Scooter behaves or this quack is going to go bananas after dealing with Scooter. OK Mr. Quack, do your thing."

As Dr. Fine was beginning to continue with Scooter, Michael, The Magnificent walked over to the table with the refreshments and started talking to Charlie, The Chill and Smitty, The Grim Reaper.

"Fellows, would you come out on the balcony with me?" asked Michael. "I need to talk to you in private."

After the three men was alone on the balcony, Michael began to say, "I asked both of you to come to this demonstration to talk to you. Dixie Doneright seems to be having two boyfriends at the same time. Dr. Preston Fine and Jerry Dickerson.

I invited Jerry Dickerson and his boys to Dr. Fine's demonstration. They should be here pretty soon. I want to hire both of you with this roll of thousand dollars to take care of Jerry Dickerson and Dixie Doneright. After Jerry gets here, bring Jerry and his boys out here on the balcony. Tell Jerry he needs to take Dixie back to the hotel and do what it takes to keep her from Dr. Fine. If he's not strong enough to talk her into staying away from Dr. Fine, he needs to use his muscles to keep her away from Dr. Fine.

Dixie is distracting our whole operation. She thinks she hasn't done anything wrong. In her case, she doesn't have to. First thing you know, she will be Dr. Fine's wife and then his manager.

If that happens, I don't want to have to deal with Jerry Dickerson. Just to make sure that doesn't happen, I suggest we work together. By working together, you can settle the score you have with Mr. Dickerson about chasing you out of town, because you wouldn't sign Smitty's boxing contract over to him."

"We're always looking for some easy money. We'll be more than glad to take care of Jerry Dickerson," insisted Charlie. "How do you want Smitty and me to do that?"

"This is how I want you to deal with Mr. Dickerson and what I want you to tell him when he gets here," explained Michael.

As the three men finished talking, they went back in to see Dr. Fine's demonstration where they saw Jerry Dickerson and his boys sitting on the other side of the room.

"Get after them," instructed Michael. Don't let them get away."

"Smitty, I don't feel good about what we're going to do. Go with me to grab Dixie first, so we can take her to Jerry Dickerson," instructed Charlie.

After Smitty and Charlie walked up to Dixie, they both grabbed each of her arms.

"We're taking you to Jerry Dickerson and then you're leaving permanently," said Charlie.

Trying to pull away from Charlie and Smitty, Dixie began to scream.

Seeing Smitty, Charlie and Dixie from the other side of the room, Stephen asked Dr. Fine to hold up on his demonstration with Scooter until he came back. Stephen then rushed over to the three of them.

"Don't do that. It's not nice to treat a lady that way. What is the problem here?" asked Stephen.

"Charlie and Smitty are trying to make me leave permanently, and I don't want to go," answered Dixie.

"What's the matter with you? Get your hands off of her and leave her be," ordered Stephen.

"What do you intend to do about it? Your asking for it. I would like to see you make me. Anytime, I'm ready," replied Smitty as he stood in front of Stephen, leading with his right hand and throwing a jab with his left, trying to hit Stephen in the face.

Stephen ducked the punch's and came back throwing a jab followed by a right cross, finished with a left hook, with an overhand right cross combination knocking Smitty on the floor.

Looking over at Charlie, Stephen asked, "Do you want some of the same?"

Holding his hands in front of his face, Charlie pleaded, "Don't hit me. Don't hit me."

"Then pick up your friend off the floor and leave Dixie alone," demanded Stephen.

"You haven't seen the last of me yet," promised Smitty.

"Any time you say. I'm The World Middle Weight Boxing Champion. The next time you bother her, I'm going to really get tough with both of you."

"Thank you sir. Thank you," said Dixie as she began to cry. "I'm glad to see you, you big dope.

"Me too, you big dope. What's going on here?" asked Columbo.

"Your like ever other cop. Your never around when the trouble starts. These two mugs here was trying to force this young lady to leave." replied Stephen.

"I thought this lady needed a friend and I'm the friendly type, so I was just explaining to these two that it was improper to treat a lady this way. I hope you didn't mind that I had to bruise one of them a little."

"It sounds like you did your good deed for the day," laughed Columbo.

"Yeah, but I'm afraid Smitty won't think so," answered Stephen.

"Why?" asked Columbo.

"Because Smitty is the one I had to bruise a little bit," replied Stephen.

"What do you think I should do with these guys?" asked Columbo.

"Call a fourth for bridge," answered Stephen.

"I didn't see a thing. I didn't get here until a couple of minutes ago." Turning to Dixie, Columbo asked, "Since these two guys was bothering you, what do you want me to do with them?"

"Call a cop," replied Dixie. "There's never a cop around when you need one."

"I am a cop. I'm Detective Columbo. Do you want to press charges against these two men?"

"No, I just want them to leave me alone. Stephen, I don't know how to show you how grateful I am," replied Dixie.

"That's quit alright. I'm glad to do what I can. That was on the house," laughed Stephen. "Here's my card. Just remember to call on me if you ever need my help."

"Are you really Stunning Stephen Edwards, The World Middle Weight Boxing Champion?," asked Dixie.

"Yes I am," replied Stephen. "I'm also a Davenport Police Detective."

"I am so embarrassed. I didn't know who you were. I'm sorry what I said to you while Dr. Fine was trying to hypnotize you," insisted Dixie.

"Don't even worry about that," answered Stephen. "That was fun."

Looking at Charlie and Smitty, Columbo asked, "Just who are you two? Show me some identification."

"I'm Charlie, The Chill and I'm Smitty, The Grim Reaper," answered both men as they pulled out their billfolds with their identification in it.

"Your kidding me. What kind of names are those?" answered Columbo.

"Smitty is a professional boxer and I'm his manager," explained Charlie. "Because boxing is our profession, we choose those names to go by."

Looking at the identification of both men, Columbo replied, "Now I remember both of you. A couple years ago, Jerry Dickerson ran you out of town due to the boxing agreement between you, because you didn't have an agreement. I'm going to let you go for now. If you bother this lady again, your going to jail. You can stay for Dr. Fine's demonstration as long as you behave yourself."

"Come on Smitty. I see somebody else we need to talk to," boomed Charlie.

"Oh yeah, I see who it is," said Smitty. "Let's go see him."

"Come on Columbo, I want to see Scooter get hypnotized," requested Stephen as some of members of the news media stopped Stephen to ask who he was.

"I'll tell you who he is," explained Columbo. "This is The World Middle Weight Boxing Champion, Stunning Stephen Edwards who is on special assignment with the police department as a Detective."

"That's a great story to go with Dr. Fine's Demonstrations," replied Joe, who was a news media member. "Mr. Edwards, would you mind answering some questions?"

"Maybe later," answered Stephen. "I'm here to watch Dr. Fine's demonstration. Right now I think we should all go over and watch Dr. Fine hypnotize my friend. That alone should make a very interesting story."

Chapter Five

DEALING WITH WRESTLING

"What are you doing here at Dr. Fine's demonstration?" asked Charlie as he approached Jerry.

"Listen, Micheal, The Magnificent, Dr. Fine's Manager just asked me to come and watch Dixie as part of the demonstration, because he knows that Dixie is my girl," answered Jerry. "What are you and Smitty doing here? The last time we saw you, we ran you out of Davenport."

"Michael, The Magnificent invited Smitty and me to see the demonstration," explained Charlie. "This demonstration was only suppose to be for the news media. I guess since we all know Dr. Fine, Michael thought we would all enjoy seeing this demonstration. Since Michael is busy with the news media, he asked Smitty and me to have a talk with you since your here. Would you and your boys come out on the balcony for that talk?"

"What would you have to talk to us about concerning Michael, The Magnificent?" asked Jerry.

"We need to talk to you in private. If you come out on the balcony, then we can talk," requested Charlie.

A minute later everybody was on the balcony.

"OK Charlie, spill it. What's so important that you have to talk to me about?" asked Jerry.

"It's about your girlfriend, Dixie," exclaimed Charlie. "Your girlfriend, Dixie is also Dr. Fine's girlfriend. She is becoming a problem with the promotion of Dr. Fine's book.

Dr. Fine can't promote his book and put on a successful demonstrations with Dixie here. She needs to go. Since she is also your girlfriend, Michael wants you to take here back to your hotel and do what it takes to keep her from coming back to Dr. Fine's Office."

"That suits me fine. That was one of the reasons I came to this demonstration," growled Jerry. "I came to get Dixie and to tell her to stay away from Dr. Fine."

"Charlie and me also want to talk to you about a business deal since you are here," proposed Smitty. "Michael doesn't know anything about this."

"There is no way we want to have a business deal with you," answered Jerry. "I always believed to beware of Greeks bearing gifts. The only thing we want to do with you is run you out of town again."

"Go ahead and do that," instructed Charlie. "Then Smitty and myself will have to go to the police and inform them that you and your cut throats are the ones who murdered that wrestler that was found dead on the roof of the hotel where you live."

"What are you trying to pull?" exclaimed Ace. "I don't want to get mixed up in murder. We didn't do that job and you know it."

"I'm sure we can convince the police that you did," laughed Charlie.

"Your going to make us suspects to a murder we didn't commit. It's a good deduction, but you couldn't sell it to a jury. We are within our rights," exclaimed Jerry. "OK, what do you want? No Games. Get right to the point. What are you expecting us to do? We want to make sure of this job."

"Charlie and myself know that since your out of the slammer, your going to come up with another illegal scheme to make some fast bucks and we want in on it," replied Smitty. "Only this time it will be our scheme and you'll be working for us."

"What are you trying to do, pull a fast one, by trying to blackmail us? No you don't. Nothing doing," insisted Jerry. "We will run you out of Davenport, before we work with you again."

"Have it your way. Smitty and myself haven't forgotten about you running us out of Davenport before and we won't forget it as long as we're alive. I guess Smitty and me will be going to the police," insisted Charlie. "Your the ones who are going to be escorted out of town, back to prison with a police escort."

"OK, you win for now. Tell me, what are you really after? Let's have it. What's the pitch?" asked Jerry. "Just what are you driving at?"

"It's like this," explained Smitty. "Since you and your boys were out of town, Charlie and myself have come up with a great idea about running a racket with the wrestlers and their managers."

"So, you're the ones who murdered the wrestler that was found dead on the roof," exclaimed Jerry. "What was you trying to do, blackmail him? Suicide inducted by black mail is murder."

"I don't want you to get the wrong idea about the wrestler," insisted Smitty. "It looks like you will find out sooner or later. Charlie and me live on the sixth floor as the same hotel as you. It may look bad for us, but Charlie and me was not responsible for the demise of the wrestler on the roof. We don't want anything to do with that murder. Then the police would be looking for us. We're just interested in making a few bucks from the wrestlers and their managers.

That's where you come in. We are pressuring the managers of these wrestlers to have their boys sign up with us. We need your help to put the screws on these managers since you already had it figured how to get the managers of the boxers to do the same. It should be as easy as smuggling pineapples into Hawaii. We also need you to protect our wrestlers. Dead wrestlers don't make us any money."

"That doesn't sound like a bad scheme," answered Jerry. "How do we know you won't turn us into the police if our partnership goes sour? I don't want to be double crossed by two small time thieves. As partners, what's our cut?"

"If we become partners, you will be able to tell the police a story about Smitty and me. That will be your insurance," answered Charlie. "I think we should divide the pie 60/40. Smitty and me naturally getting 60, since we developed this racket."

"I disapprove. I say we divide the pie 50/50, since me and the boys are very experienced in these matters," demanded Jerry. "Ace, Lefty, stay by the door. I don't want our new partners to leave in a hurry."

"What are we going to do Jerry?" asked Ace.

"Now that Smitty and Charlie has had their say in this business deal, I'm going to tell them how our business deal is really going to be run," explained Jerry. "I am going to be the boss and I want more money. Smitty and Charlie, you are going to be working for me. I agree we will divide the pie 60/40, only I will be getting 60 per cent. If you run to the police, you better keep on running. If you decide to agree to my terms, I'm sure I can make you more money than your making now. If I make a deal with you, I won't go back on my word."

"Smitty, what do you think we should do?" asked Charlie.

"I guess work the deal like Jerry wants," replied Smitty. "You and I wasn't doing too bad with this racket. I vote we work with Jerry."

"OK Jerry, it looks like we're going to be partners on your terms," offered Charlie.

"You sure changed your mind in a hurry. Did this turn out to be a spur of the moment idea," questioned Jerry. "Or did you forget something?"

"No boss, the conditions of the deal made sense," reasoned Smitty.

"Now that we have an agreement for a deal, tell me what your room number is?" requested Jerry.

"Our room number is 6015," answered Charlie. "What is your room number?"

"My room number is 5025," replied Jerry. "Now I want to go in and see Dr. Fine's demonstration, before I miss it."

"All right boss," replied Charlie. "Smitty and I are also anxious to see the demonstration."

After Charlie and Smitty returned from the balcony, Michael walked up to them and asked, "How did it go with Jerry?"

"It worked just like you wanted," answered Smitty. "Jerry took it hook, line and sinker."

"That takes care of the first part of my plan," explained Michael. "I want to talk to you later about the second part of my plan."

Chapter Six

Dr. Fine Continues With Scooter

As the men returned from the balcony, Dr. Fine is waiting for Stephen and Columbo to return so he could continue his demonstration with Scooter.

As Stephen returned, he said to Dr. Fine, "I'm sorry to inconvenience you, but Dixie Doneright was in a bad spot."

"What was those two men doing with Dixie?" asked Dr. Fine.

"You have several people waiting to see your demonstration with Scooter. Go ahead with it and I'll tell you later," requested Stephen.

"Scooter has an excellent head. The question remains what it contains. OK, let's continue," mumbled a nervous Dr. Fine. "Scooter you are under my power. Don't move. Listen to me, only me and nobody else. Your getting sleepy, very sleepy. You will sleep deeper and deeper. With one short step, I'm going to take you back to a long journey in time. Let's go back, back, back."

"Mommy, my diapers need changing. Feed me," wailed Scooter.

"You don't have to cry little Scooter. We'll get your mommy to take care of you. While we're waiting for your mommy, let's go back further in time. I'm going to take you back to another time, to another to another place, to another life when you was somebody else," instructed Dr. Fine. "Tell me just what comes from your heart. Where are you now? Who are you?"

"I'm a Deputy Marshal in Dodge City Kansas. The date is 1880," explained Scooter. "Before I was a Deputy Marshal, I was a bartender at Belle's Saloon. I got a girl. Her name is Clara belle and she owns the saloon. I do a lot of stupid things. She wouldn't even tell me to shut up when I didn't say anything that wasn't smart and she still liked me.

One day when I was working as a bartender in Bell's Saloon, three cowboys came in. I said to them, what will you have? The first cowboy answered that he wanted a whiskey. So I turned around to get the bottle of whiskey off the shelf behind me and poured him a drink. The other two cowboys didn't say anything, so I put the bottle of whiskey back on the shelf.

Then I turned around and asked the other two cowboys if they wanted something to drink? The second cowboy answered that he would like a whiskey. I again turned around and grabbed the bottle of whiskey off of the shelf and poured him a drink. Then I asked the third cowboy if he wanted a glass of whiskey. He answered no, so I put the bottle of whiskey back on the shelf.

After that I then turned around and asked the third cowboy what he wanted to drink?

He answered that he wanted two glasses of whiskey. I then turned around and grabbed the whiskey off of the shelf, grabbed an empty glass and started repeatedly pouring whiskey in the glass and throwing the whiskey in the faces of the cowboys, until the bottle of whiskey was empty.

My girl Clara Belle watched from the top of the stairs as the cowboys was soaked full of whiskey. Clara Belle then rushed down the stairs to apologize to the cowboys and then told me to look for another job.

Next I got the job as a Deputy of Marshal Allen. Right now I'm looking for Marshal Allen. Where is Marshal Allen? I've got to find Marshal Allen."

"Why do you need to find Marshal Allen?" asked a puzzled Dr. Fine. "You look for him every where in Dodge, but you can't find him. Where are you now?"

"I got word that The Stunning Kid was coming to Dodge. I'm on the edge of Dodge City. A masked rider is coming toward me.

Here he comes. It's The Stunning Kid," continued Scooter. "One day as I was walking past the bank, I looked through the window and saw everybody standing there with their hands up. I went inside the bank to find out what was going on. The Stunning Kid was standing in front of the line with his guns out. That's when I found out how polite he was, because he let everybody in front of him by walking to the back of the line so he could rob the bank. After all the bank's money and the customer's money was put in a sack, The Stunning Kid thanked everybody and left.

It seems that The Stunning Kid can never kill or inflict pain enough. It was the job of The Marshal and me to catch him because he's a thief and a murderer. After The Stunning Kid is put behind bars, Dodge City Kansas is going to be a deceit city to live in again.

The Marshal had a saying that goes, "He thought it was funny to steel someones money. It's better to be safe than sorry, because if he gets reckless, we'll give him a necklace that is tied to a tree. Then he will be finding out that crime doesn't pay, because we'll be throwing dirt in his face."

It was just my luck to catch up with him alone. I wanted to run, but my legs wasn't cooperating. I said to myself, "I have to get out of here, but how? I've got no choice but to reach for my gun and I draw.

The funny thing is there is no gun in my holster. It turned out to be a round can of pepper in my holster instead of my gun. I begin to yell at The Stunning Kid not to hurt me as he draws both of his guns. Then I shake the can of pepper and with a lot of luck with pepper going into the eyes of The Stunning Kid.

After that I had the confidence of a small boy at the dentist, after the tooth was pulled. I yelled, I got him! I got him! I almost got The Stunning Kid, but then it looked like he almost got me. Then I see my chance and I start to run away from The Stunning Kid yelling for Marshal Allen to help me."

"Did you get away from The Stunning Kid? Why did he want to kill you?" inquired Dr. Fine. "Did You find Marshal Allen?"

"What a dumb question. Of course I didn't get away from the Stunning Kid. The Stunning Kid killed me. After that I found

Marshal Allen at Bell's Saloon in a back room drunk as a skunk," answered Scooter. "I asked the Marshal why he was so drunk?"

"Did you have any idea what he was trying to say?" asked Dr. Fine.

"Marshal Allen replied in a drunken manner," Scooter went on to say, "What do you think, you moron? I just want to get out of this job. You're always trying to take advantage of me. Every time I turn my back, nothing gets done. You won't listen to me and learn the procedures of being a Deputy Marshal and because of that you destroyed the evidence we had on The Stunning Kid.

You're always embarrassing me. Whenever you're in trouble, you never call on me. A week ago, you told me that you tracked down fifty Indians by yourself that jumped the reservation. You're always doing something stupid, because you was like an optimist and instead saw a doughnut. You thought the best way to capture the Indians was to surround them. Then you told me that was a bad idea, because then you was like a pessimist. You began to see the hole in the doughnut, because they killed you."

"Oh that?" replied Scooter. "I thought you knew I was like a cat with nine lives. By the way, what other animal has more than one life?"

"A drunken Marshal, because he's always in a dead state of drunkenness due to a stupid Deputy Marshal," answered Marshal Allen.

"Nice try. You are absolutely wrong. Survey says the true number one answer is a frog, because he croaks every night," answered Scooter as everybody began laughing.

"Rex, Columbo, Dr. Fine is going to be surprised when he finds out that Scooter going back in time is really a dream Stephen had," laughed Hannibal.

"That was some of my dream. Most of the story he told Dr. Fine, he made up and it is a good one," laughed Stephen.

"OK Scooter, when I count to three, you will wake up," instructed Dr. Fine. "One, two, three, you can wake up now. I said you can wake up."

After Scooter woke, he demanded, "When are you going to hypnotize Stephen? I haven't got all day you know. What am I doing sitting in this chair? I was standing behind the chair. Now I'm sitting in it. How did I get here?"

"Dr. Fine hypnotized you and then you was moved to the chair," laughed Stephen.

"I had the strangest dream. It was a very funny dream," reasoned Scooter.

"While you was hypnotized you were repeating a dream Stephen had a couple of years ago. Most of what you told Dr. Fine you made up about Stephen's dream. Dr. Fine didn't take you back in time. He just thought he did," laughed Hannibal.

"Well, I'm a monkey's uncle," laughed Scooter.

"Quite, the news media is here to cover the story. Do you want everyone to know that your a monkey's uncle?" teased Hannibal.

"Ooh, ooh, ooh, me and my big mouth," replied Scooter. "I would certainly get rid of it, only I think it's a handy place to keep my teeth."

"I remember Stephen's dream," chimed in Columbo.

"That was quite a dream Stephen had," boomed Rex. "Dr. Fine, we warned you about Scooter. That was a very interesting demonstration, but I'm afraid you missed the bus. You really didn't do anything. I told you this was going to be a wild goose chase. It was just as I figured that it would turn out that Scooter was going to have you in his power. I've seen enough gang. I think we better go."

"That demonstration will make a very good story to write," beamed Joe from the news media.

"No, wait, don't print that story. It's a mystery to me as to what happened. I must be slipping. Let me try hypnotizing Scooter again. I can't be right all the time," exclaimed Dr. Fine.

"Wishful thinking will lead to a blind alley when you're dealing with Scooter," promised Hannibal.

"The door of opportunity swings both ways. Wishful thinking can be fulfilled. I've got the power and I know I can take Scooter back in time and pass him from one body into another," insisted Dr. Fine.

"Well, goody for you," laughed Stephen. "You don't fool anybody. For you to admit that you failed is like drinking sour milk."

"Leave me alone. As far as I'm concerned, it's like buying sandwiches from a fast food restaurant. After I eat my sandwiches, I don't care what I do with the wrappers and the sack. I don't want to do anything with you. You can't hypnotize me again. My mind is a blank," objected Scooter. "Shut up. Don't say it."

"That's nothing new, but that is very smart thinking. That's exactly how I had it figured out. Your brain really amazes me, but it's really nothing. We all know that your mind is a blank," laughed Hannibal.

"I think we all have seen enough. Margret, now do you understand why I wanted to bring Scooter?" asked Rex. "Dr. Fine can't do what he says he can do. Scooter just saved us $500.00. I think we better go."

"But Rex, what about me?" asked Margret. "Can't we stay and let Dr. Fine hypnotize me?"

"No Margret, I just told you Dr. Fine can't help you," answered Rex. "Wasn't you listening to a word said?"

"I believe I really can help your wife. Give me a chance," requested Dr. Fine. "If it's the money you're worrying about, I will take the liberty to do the first one for free?"

"Some other time Dr. Fine. It's time for us to go," repeated Rex. "Margret, why don't you go home? Stephen, Hannibal and Scooter, would you go back to the station. I want to talk to all of you again about Jerry Dickerson."

"Are you going to make me go in the ring and box Ace The Assassin again?" asked Scooter.

"If Scooter has to box Ace, will I have to be invisible again?" asked Stephen. "I sure would like to do that again. I really like to box. Being invisible is even more fun while I'm boxing."

"No it's nothing like that," answered Rex. "Wait until we get back to my office where we can talk in private."

"It's a good thing for Ace that I don't have to box him again," roared Scooter. "I would really tear him from limb to limb like I did last time. I would break both of his arms. I would knock out all his teeth."

"Scooter, stop it you lunk head!" yelled Hannibal as he raised his hand ready to hit Scooter. "You hid behind Stephen when he was invisible while you were in the ring, because you was scared stiff of Ace. Now get out of my sight."

"Help Stephen, save me! Make me invisible" cried Scooter as he hid behind Stephen. "Old habits never die."

"Boys don't get riled. I want you boys stop it," ordered Columbo.

"Hannibal, I thought I told you to quit treating Scooter this way," scolded Stephen.

"Even though Scooter is my best friend, he makes me so mad acting like a lam brained idiot," explained Hannibal. "Scooter, I'm sorry."

"You better apologize," replied Scooter looking at Hannibal from behind Stephen. "Now I don't have to hurt you."

"Come on boys. Let's get back to the station," repeated Rex.

"Why don't you go without me?" requested Scooter. "I want to go talk to a friend of mine who is standing across the room. His name is Joe and I went to high school with him. Now he is with the news media."

"Go ahead Scooter. We will wait here for you. Don't be to long," offered Rex. "I need all of you to back at the station at the same time. I need all of your help in this matter. That's why Stephen came back to the Quad Cities. To help Columbo and me."

Scooter immediately turned and walked over to Joe.

"Hi Joe, when did you start?" asked Scooter.

"I got this job after I graduated from," replied Joe.

"How long have you been?" inquired Scooter.

"Oh for a couple of years," explained Joe. "What have you and The West Side Kids?"

"We went to The University Of Davenport and are now," Scooter informed Joe.

"How do you like being?" inquired Joe.

"I always wanted to," answered Scooter.

"What kind of jobs do?" asked Joe.

"We have been working with two Davenport Police Detectives and have some interesting," explained Scooter

"That sounds like a fun job," replied Joe. "How did you get?"

"We bought The Detective agency from Detective Murphy," answered Scooter. "My friends are waiting for me over there and I have to."

"It was good to see you. We'll have to talk again some time," insisted Joe. "I can't believe how much you had to say."

"We'll do that. I always like to hear what you have to say. I have to go now," answered Scooter as Dr. Fine asks everybody to be seated.

Chapter Seven

The Supreme Demonstration Of Murder

"Quite, please. Quite please. May I have everybody's attention?" insisted Dr. Fine to the audience. "It looks like we have a full house, so now it's time for our supreme demonstration of excellence that can be achieved by a young lady. Now I'm going to introduce this very charming and mysterious young lady to you who is going to charm the audience by assisting me in this demonstration. I want you to meet the worlds most living great mind reader under hypnotist, Dixie Doneright."

After Dixie sat down in a chair, Dr. Fine asked for absolute quit again.

Talking to Dixie, Dr. Fine began to say, "Dixie, close your eyes and keep them closed. You are getting sleepy, very sleepy. You will sleep deeper, deeper, deeper. Now you are under my power. You will listen to nobody else but me. I'm going to start with my first question and I'm not going to make it easy."

Then Dr. Fine approached one of the reporters in the audience and asked for his ring. Holding the ring in the air, Dr. Fine asked Dixie, "What am I holding in my hand?"

"It's a gold ring," replied Dixie. "Their is an inscription inside the ring that says To My Teddy Bear."

"That's absolutely right, Dixie," replied Dr. Fine.

Dr. Fine then asked a second reporter for his watch. Holding the watch in the air Dr. Fine asked, "Dixie, what do I have in my right hand? Take your time. Take your time to answer."

"Your holding in your hand a wrist watch," answered Dixie.

"Right again," replied Dr. Fine.

Dr. Fine then walked over to Margret and asked her to whisper in his ear the question that fills her mind.

"Somebody whispered something in my ear," hinted Dr. Fine. "Who was it and what was I asked?"

"It was Margret Tarillo and she asked you when you was going to hypnotize her," answered Dixie.

"That's very uncanny. Right again," repeated Dr. Fine.

"Now who am I pointing at?" asked Dr. Fine as he walked over to Stephen Edwards.

"You are pointing at The World Middle Weight Boxing Champion, Stunning Stephen Edwards," answered Dixie.

"Dixie, you are right again," yelled Dr. Fine. "Now let's do something really hard.

Stephen, whisper in my ear why you are really here?

Dixie, tell us what Stephen said to me. Do you have a message for Stephen? What are you going to tell him?"

"Do you believe in astrology? Can you tell me, is Scorpio the unfortunate symbol of death? What can you tell me about Dr. Zodiac is what Stephen asked," answered Dixie.

"Stunning Stephen Edwards, you have a restless mind. You are a fellow that is faced with certain death?" insisted Dixie. "Before it's too late, I think there is something you should know. Dr. Zodiac knows all things about all people. Do not challenge the supernatural, unless you are prepared to die. I can't go on. There is evil here in this room. There is a killer among us who is thinking of murder. I never laid eyes on him before."

"What kind of demonstration is this? Can't anybody talk about anything but murder?" screamed Margret Tarillo.

At that moment the lights went out and Dixie began to scream, "Who turned out the lights?"

Twenty seconds later, the lights were turned back on. On the floor laid Joe, one of the journalists. Seeing Joe on the floor, Rex and Columbo rushed over to Joe. With a quick inspection Rex announced to everyone that Joe was dead. He had a poisonous dart sticking out of the back of his neck.

"Joe was killed with a poison dart that is sticking out of the back of his neck." observed Rex. "Well, it's all over for him. He was very neatly murdered and now he's permanently dead. Nobody is to leave the scene of the crime. We have to suspect everybody on general principle.

Well this is a surprise. Jerry Dickerson, what are you doing here? Fancy finding you here. I really wasn't expecting to see you here. What did you steel today?"

"I didn't steel anything. What's the matter, aren't you glad to see me? I don't want to violate my parole and go back to jail," replied Jerry. "Since Dr. Fine worked for us before I went to jail, Michael, The Magnificent was kind enough to invited me and my boys here to see his demonstration."

"I didn't see your name on the guest list," insisted Rex.

"Of course not. I'm using my maiden name," explained Jerry.

"What about that. Since you're all conveniently here, I want to interview all of you about a wrestler that was killed, murdered on the roof of the hotel where you stay at," insisted Rex.

"Rex, how are we going to work this investigation?" asked Columbo. "Say, that girl came in handy on this. Do you think the girl is in on this?"

"I don't know. I can't figure her out. Stephen and I will talk to Jerry and his boys on this side of the room," answered Rex. "You, Hannibal and Scooter, take the others and move to the other side of the room and interview them."

"OK, everybody move to this side of the room and sit down. Everybody sit down and be patient. Now, I need to find out what anybody saw," Columbo started to say to his group of people. "Did anybody see anything suspicious? Any witness to this crime may be in great danger. You may think that it is better to see and not tell, not here, not now. I wish somebody would tell me that they saw something so we can destroy the web of the spider. After that is done, we can look for the spider. We need to remove his disguise to find out who he is."

"I know who it was," insisted Scooter. "It was a ghost with a knife."

"No Scooter. You're quite wrong," corrected Columbo. "Somebody here has a blow gun. I want to find out who it is."

As Columbo was interviewing his group, Stephen and Rex began to interview Jerry and his boys.

"Since you are all conveniently here at Dr. Fine's, I want to talk to all of you to help prevent another murder," Rex began to say. "We must talk to you about both murders to see what you know."

"OK boys, let's cooperate with The Detective. We didn't have anything to do with any murder," exclaimed Jerry. "We don't want to go back to the slammer. That idiot that calls himself a Detective has to interview all of us. He really is a stupid Detective, because there was a man murdered here under his eyes. Now he's like a blood hound on the trail of that murderer. That's the only way he can keep his job."

"Before we get started, I want to inform all of you to leave your hands off of Stunning Stephen Edwards," demanded Rex. "Not only is Stephen The World Middle Weight Boxing Champion, he is now a Police Detective. If any of you mess with or threaten Stephen, I will personally see that you go back to the slammer. Is that understood?"

"How about I challenge Stephen to a boxing match?" broke in Ace. "It would give me great pleasure to legally beat him up and take that championship belt away from him. The only way he can beat me is when he's invisible. I would like to get in the ring with him and fight him again when I can see him. He's afraid to fight me when I can see him and he knows it."

"That's between you and Stephen to take care of later," replied Rex. "Were looking for information, anything that is useful in solving the case about the wrestler who was found dead on the roof of the hotel you are staying at.

I want to warn all of you to be ready for trouble. The killer may be living in the same hotel as you. I don't want him to take pot shot at you. When he was last seen, he had brown hair and a mustache. Now he be hiding behind a mask. What I mean to say is that he may have had his face changed by a Doctor Miles to remain invisible, to cheat the law.

The killer is a master criminal who is very deceitful. He is known for the face he hides behind. You remember a fellow called Detective Murphy? You know him as Detective Justin Murphy."

"What ever happened to him?" asked Ace.

"He's disappeared. He's around somewhere. He's wanted for robbery and murder. We believe that Detective Murphy lives somewhere in your hotel. Everyone who lives in your hotel is in danger with this killer on the loose," replied Rex.

"How can this be Detective Murphy?" asked Jerry. "Are you sure that's really him? He was really a defective detective. He couldn't possibly go from a detective to a master criminal. He's not very smart to be deceitful, let alone a master criminal. We ran him out of town so easy. He ran so fast that he didn't take time to look back."

"After you went to jail, Detective Murphy's mind must have snapped and he became very evil," answered Rex. "He was convicted of a couple brutal murders and was very hard to catch. Now you know as much about it as I do."

"Charlie, The Chill and Smitty, The Grim Reaper, can you explain your presence here?" asked Stephen."It seems that Jerry and his boys chased you out of Davenport just like they did Detective Murphy. What are you doing here at Dr. Fine's demonstration with Jerry?"

"We were invited here to see the demonstration by Michael, The Magnificent, Dr. Fine's manager," replied Jerry.

As Jerry finished talking, Rex looked over at Margret sitting in a chair. Knowing Margret's mental condition, Rex rushed over to Margret to see how she was feeling. As he was standing their looking at Margret, he could see that she was suffering from mental shock.

"Columbo, Stephen, would you come here? This has been quite an ordeal for Margret," yelled Rex. "Margret isn't feeling a bit good."

"I'm sorry if I seem upset," cried Margret.

"I don't blame you for what you've been through," reassured Rex. "Columbo, would you and Stephen continue the investigation of the murdered man? I have to take Margret home."

"Can Scooter and myself help you with Margret?" asked Hannibal.

"No Hannibal, I can manage Margret," answered Rex. "You and Scooter stay here and help Columbo. Good luck boys. Come on Margret, let's go home."

"May I be of some assistance to you? Are you having any trouble?" asked Michael, The Magnificent.

"Who are you," answered Rex.

"After I explain to you what my professional name is and what I can do, maybe you would like me to take care of the complication with this beautiful lady, poor soul, she is just too highly strung?" Michael went on to say. "Let's go out on the balcony where we can talk in private."

"Hannibal, would you stay with Margret until I come back?" requested Rex.

"Don't worry, Rex. I will take good care of Margret," replied Hannibal. "Scooter, you help Uncle Columbo."

Once out on the balcony, Michael, The Magnificent began to say, "My professional name is Dr. Nejino. Seeing Margret from a distance, I can tell she is a lady in distress due to being a highly strung imaginative woman with a lot of anxiety. I call it a severe think ability. I help woman with these mental problems all the time. That's what I'm here for. Do you want to hear some more?" asked Michael.

"I don't know what to say," said a puzzled Rex. "Go on. I'm all ears."

"As long as I know what's going to happen, I can prevent it. To relieve this anxiety when they don't calm down I deal in spooks. The reason I deal in spooks is the foundation of my method. It helps these women get out of the world of reality. It will calm their nerves where they don't have a worry or a care. Sometimes we need fantasy to get out of the world of reality.

I don't believe in spooks myself. Would you like to bring her to east of 6th and Gaines, where I have a large home on top of the hill east of that intersection, to get one of my treatments? Normally I get $500.00 a treatment. I will do the first one for free."

"I don't know what to say," said a puzzled Rex. "I have to talk this over with Margret and then I will let you know. Give me one of your business cards and then I better take Margret home. If Margret and me decide you can help her, I will call you. Columbo, Stephen, would you come here?"

"What do you want?" asked Columbo as he approached Rex.

"I want you to meet Michael, The Magnificent. He is Dr. Fine's manager," answered Rex. "He also has an alias and is know as Dr. Nejino. For your information, Dr. Nejino believes in an after world. Dr. Nejino says he can talk to the spirits. In other words, he works with ghosts and uses them in his work to treat women with their anxiety.

We don't have anything to go on right now. Maybe you can use him with his ghosts to give us some clues in this investigation. It doesn't make much sense how he works. Maybe he can help. You must use all the resources you have to find a way to bring this evil doer to justice. I don't want any more killings. Come on Margret. Let's go home."

Chapter Eight

DETECTIVE STUNNING STEPHEN EDWARDS TAKES OVER

After Rex and Margret left, Stephen said to Columbo, "Well, where do we go from here? What are we going to do next?"

"I don't know yet," answered Columbo.

"I've got an idea how to proceed with this investigation. Is it OK with you if I try out my idea?" asked Stephen.

"At this moment everything is a mystery to me. We have to start someplace," replied Columbo. "Stephen, if you you have an idea how to get the solution to this murder, go ahead if you want to try it."

"Don't worry. I'll handle this. I've got everything covered. OK everybody, go back to where you was originally seated before the lights went out," instructed Stephen. "Hannibal, Scooter, stand by the switches for the lights. Columbo, look for anything suspicious.

I am convinced that the young lady, Dixie Doneright can be assistance to us. I also asked Michael, The Magnificent, alias Dr. Nejino to help. With Dixie Doneright's strange power of her mental skills and Dr. Nejino's spooks, combine with our scientific investigation, working together it may to help solve this murder. If we penetrate Dixie's mind, we may find the solution to this crime. Dr. Fine will be hypnotizing Dixie again."

"OK Dixie, now that your sitting in the same chair as you did before the lights went out, let's begin," requested Dr. Fine. "I want complete silence from everybody as we begin again. There is great danger in what we are all about to see and hear. I must warn all of you that death is present. Dixie's body can play no part as to what happens. The spirits will take over Dixie's body completely.

Dixie, I want you to close your eyes and listen only to my voice as you did before. I want you to sleep, sleep, sleep. Sleep deeper like you did before. Ask Joe to appear."

"Joe's spirit is crying out," Dixie began to say. "There is a barrier in the way. I will try and remove the barrier. Joe are you there? Are you from another world? Hello Joe, we need you Joe. You can't be far away. What are you waiting for? Come back and explain your untimely death. The police here in this room is trying to solve a murder, your murder. Don't go away Joe. The unbelievers must know that a spirit is trying to get through. It's the spirit of Joe. Joe I command you to speak," insisted Dixie. "Take over my mind body and soul. My lips will speak your thoughts as they come to you. Speak, you unhappy spirit.

This is what Joe's ghost is saying," explained Dixie. "Joe would like us to know sometimes it's better to see and not tell. Joe says that he was killed due to a story he was writing. Joe was writing a story about organized blackmail on illegal wrestling. Another reporter named Richard was working with Joe on that story.

Tell us, Who has the blow gun? Who is the killer? Give us some ideas?" asked Dixie.

"Why take up my time when you already know the answer?" replied Joe.

"The Doctor has a message for Stunning Stephen Edwards. Be aware: Scorpio is the unfortunate symbol of death. You are in danger. You must leave Davenport and never come back."

"I see a dark cloud, evil, menacing. Watch out! There is something getting in the way, something evil. He's here in this room and he's going to strike again! I can see his face and I know who he is. It's, it's Dr. Zodiac. What's your racket? I don't think I've ever seen you

46

around. You are an insane person with evil in you're heart!" screamed Dixie as the lights went out again.

"I've never been around. Do you really think I'm insane? I don't have any friends. The only friend I have is myself," laughed Dr. Zodiac. "When you don't believe in the supernatural, death is your reward. Detective Stunning Stephen Edwards, your next."

"Alright, come out wise guy," ordered Stephen.

Thirty seconds later the lights were back on. There was not a trace of Dr. Zodiac to be seen anywhere. He was gone, clean as a whistle. This time, Richard was laying on the floor with a poisoned dart in his neck.

Jerry immediately rushed over to see who was down on the floor.

"Hey. Something is wrong. I hope it's not bad news. Is he dead?" asked Columbo.

"Yes, he is another one. He's out like a ton of lead. He won't give anybody any more trouble, because he's out of the way for keeps," answered Jerry.

"Does anybody know who he was?" questioned Columbo.

"I wouldn't know,"admitted Jerry. "Your the Detective."

"It was Richard who was working with Joe. What do you know about this murder?

What are you doing here? What are you looking for?" asked Columbo.

"This is murder. If you are shielding someone by aiding or abiding a criminal or are Dr. Zodiac, your going back to jail," explained Stephen. "If I can prove that you broke the law, I'm going to box your ears off. I'm not playing games."

"You have to come again. Why, what do you mean? Watch your language chum," warned Ace. "I don't like mysterious words."

"What's the idea? What right do you have to ask me if I'm Dr. Zodiac?" boomed Jerry. "What are you trying to do? Are you insinuating that I killed these men? When I looked on the floor, Richard was already dead. That doesn't give you the right to check everything I do. I don't like your attitude. What right do you have to cross examine me?"

"I wasn't aiming to," answered Stephen.

"What are you trying to say? Are you calling me a liar?" asked Jerry.

"I'll tell you what I think. You've already crossed yourself up twice by standing over the body. You can figure the rest out for yourself," replied Stephen. "Someone was sitting behind both of these men. They didn't have a chance. You and your gang was sitting behind both men who was murdered here tonight. I think you are Dr. Zodiac and you murdered them. You can't tell me how Dr. Zodiac got away because you're him. You're the killer. I think you may be working with some one else. If you're not Dr. Zodiac, it would make sense for you to work together"

"Is that so. Well pal, you're talking through your cheap hat. That can't be true. Because I didn't do it, you can't prove I did it," replied Jerry.

"Stop being coy. What are you hiding? You're like a man with a toupee, because you're both trying to cover up," answered Stephen. "Don't tell me what I can see with my own eyes. I have the one grain of luck that I need for an air tight case against you. It's worth a whole corn field of wisdom, because I'm afraid I can prove it."

"Did you stage this whole thing?" asked Columbo.

"Yes Columbo, I did," explained Stephen. "I set a trap to catch the killer, but I wasn't planing for someone else to die. Now I know I have the right man and I know I can prove it."

"Oh no you don't wise guy. Just a minute. Why are you accusing me of a crime I didn't commit? You think your very clever. It looks like your playing a game with me," insisted Jerry. "You just don't have any sentiment. You think you are going to prove that I'm the killer, because I was after you for not taking a fall in your boxing match. These are baseless accusations and prejudice about a grudge.

I don't like being the stumbling block. You sure seem to be confused, yet you think you are holding the aces. In fact I think you are really confused as to who killed these men. I would run away if I was guilty. Don't worry. I know I'll never get anywhere running away."

"You was put in prison for the crimes you committed, due to boxing. I think you graduated to murder since they let you out of prison. The fingerprints on the poison darts may have the message I need and it will give you away. I only have part of the proof. When I find that blow gun, I will prove your the killer," promised Stephen. "You don't fool me with those little wheels spinning around in your head."

"Why don't you listen to those little wheels? Maybe they will tap out what I'm thinking in code," replied Jerry. "Well, here we go again. It looks like were the favorite suspects of the police again. You think you're making a case against us. Well boys, it looks like we're in one of our usual jams with the police. Every time someone is knocked off in this room, we get the rap for it. What kind of cops are you, anyway?"

"You asked for it and you got it," boomed Stephen. "OK, let's put it this way. It doesn't look good for you. I'm not missing a bet that you're up to your neck in this."

"We don't like to be imposed on. Say, what are you trying to put over on us?" asked Jerry. "Just because we're standing over a corpse with a room full of cops, it doesn't mean we're guilty."

"Jerry, your not going to disappoint us with some of your double talk. I suppose you're going to tell me you was just sitting on you're front porch when this happened. That won't wash. You don't have a front porch since you are living in a hotel. Why don't you come clean? I'm going to give you a chance to save that neck of yours," demanded Stephen.

"You may think this is one of the easiest jobs you have tackled. This may not be as easy as you think. It seems you want to do this the hard way. Let me show you an easier way. Tell me, how does all this work? Don't you see. Look, I'm going to give you a chance. It's the only chance you have. Aren't you rather being foolish?"

"That's OK. I've been foolish all my life. You evidently know the whole story. Yet you want me to act as if I was a criminal making a confession," replied Jerry. "Sorry, I don't have any blow gun or pop gun. I was just sitting here watching my girlfriend, Dixie being hypnotized like everyone else. I had no idea that she could read minds after being hypnotized. Every time I see her, she sends me."

"Would you like to try another story? I know I have the right man," insisted Stephen. "If we did catch you with the blow gun, I'm sure you would say you didn't use it to kill anyone. You just carry it around for balance. I know I have the right man and I'll prove your the killer. Your know your not being very smart. Now tell me. What happened?"

"What's the matter fellow? Are you positive you can prove that I am the killer? That would be an absolute waste of time, because I don't know what happened. It's going to be a shock to you, because I did nothing wrong. You can't prove I'm the killer," reasoned Jerry.

"That's the wrong thing to say. I know better than to trust an old liar like you. Your mouth is like a lock, when you keep your mouth shut, you keep the right things locked in and the wrong things out," Stephen went on to say. "You want us to believe that this killing is going to be very difficult, very mysterious to solve and these two killings was just a coincidence. Accidents don't happen like this in one night. You're leading with your chin. Now talk."

"Oh cut it out you clutter brain, We would prefer to listen, only we don't like your tone you have with Jerry," exclaimed Ace. "You have no right to say that to Jerry. Why pick on him? You hate the truth and you know it!"

"It is a shame and very unfortunate for the men who was murdered here tonight," scolded Stephen.

"It's unfortunate for you. After the miserable mess you made out of this case, you are more like the Keystone Cops and are hardly qualify as experts, because two men were killed before your eyes," exclaimed Ace. "You clowns couldn't find a wiener on a hot dog stand. You've been everything but efficient in this case.

Columbo, what did you ever do to deserve an assistant like Stephen? He seems mad about something. I think he's mad at us and is trying to take Jerry and the rest of us down because of what happened between him and us in boxing."

"I want to remind you that you are talking to a Police Detective," replied Stephen. "See this badge. I'm the law."

"Don't put on any air's with me just because you have that badge," answered Ace. "None of us wants to go back to jail and loose all that free air, especially for something we didn't do. I don't want to go to jail. All I want to do is box. Since Stephen is trying to pin the rap on us and now he is a Detective, I can't pin his ears back without getting arrested. Now I really want to get in the ring with Stephen. Stephen may not be afraid of anybody, but he isn't as tough as he thinks he is. What I intend to do is pin his ears back and do this legally. When I'm done with Mr. Stunning Stephen, he is going to want to leave town voluntarily. The next time you work with another Detective make sure he knows what he is doing."

"I'm sorry if you feel that way about me Ace. I want to remind you, Columbo and I are still in charge of this case," explained Stephen. "Do you mind if I conduct the investigation my way? You don't give me much credit for resourcefulness, do you? When this is all over with and your not in jail, I would gladly meet you in the ring. I really want to find out if you're as tough as you claim to be or just a wind bag that's all mouth."

"Why you. I ought to let you have it now!" yelled Ace.

"Calm down Ace," demanded Jerry. "We're going to get out of this jam, even if we have to help poor Detective Stephen to solve this case ourselves. Then you'll have your day with Stephen in the ring if he doesn't back out from boxing you, because he's afraid."

"Don't worry Jerry. I'm not afraid of Ace and I'm definitely am not going to back out," replied Stephen. "I can't touch Ace legally here without cause. What I ought to do is to go over to the table and get Ace a glass of punch and really give it to him. When I get Ace in the ring, I will be hitting him so hard, when I'm through with him, he won't remember his name.

Now if it isn't too much trouble Jerry, would you like to come to the station so we can ask you and your boys some more questions?"

"I'm afraid we'll have to come with you. Because you have that badge you showed us, I guess it makes you're the law," replied Jerry.

"Hannibal, Scooter, keep an eye on Jerry and his mob," instructed Stephen. "I'm going to call the station and have them send up a couple of squad cars over to pick Jerry and his crew up. Don't let them try anything funny."

"It's funny enough around here already," laughed Jerry.

"I bet I can do that right," promised Scooter. "It's a safe bet that they are as secure as sardines in a can."

"Stephen, I'm going to call for two ambulances to take these two dead men to the morgue," added Columbo. "After we make these calls, let's get everybody's name, phone number, e-mail, home address and who they work for. Then let them go.

We also need to get the lab here to look for evidence. I'm sure we have the killers here. Jerry, because we can't prove anything, this doesn't clear you of murder. In the absence of evidence to support our claim, we have to let you go."

"Boy, is that good. That's mighty decent of you Columbo. Do you really mean it that you're going to let us go?" beamed Jerry. "Are you sure? What's the catch?"

"You win. I can't prove anything. I have nothing on you and I have to let you go. That's the best I can do, so scram," replied Columbo.

"If you mean that Columbo, that's good enough for me," answered Jerry. "You're a pal. Thank you again. I knew I could count on you."

"Next we have to talk to Dr. Fine, Dixie and Michael, The Magnificent to see what they know. Maybe Dixie, with her talents can tell us more," reasoned Columbo. "The best way to find a rabbit's residence is to turn him loose. Now that Jerry is gone, ask Hannibal and Scooter to tail him. Jerry is no fool and he may think he's going to be hard to tail.

He's better for us out of jail instead of in jail. I want more evidence and I'm going to get it. Ace just made one slip up. Another false move and we'll have him."

"What do you mean that Ace made a slip up?" asked Scooter.

"I know exactly what your Uncle Columbo is talking about," explained Stephen. "I noticed Ace was tapping his foot. He was talking to Jerry in Morse Code. He asked Jerry if they were all going back to his apartment at the hotel. Jerry replied to Ace by shaking his head yes. Since you and Hannibal know where Jerry is going, Just keep an eye on him and his gang."

I'm sure the media has stories to write and report. I want to talk to them before you let them go. If we don't find Dr. Zodiac, there may be some changes in our department." reasoned Columbo.

"I wouldn't worry about that," reassured Stephen. "I think we're getting closer to Dr. Zodiac every minute. I want all the news media to gather round. Detective Columbo wants to talk to you before you go."

"Between you, the news media and me, we have had a good understanding," explained Columbo. "May I have the cooperation of all of you? I know the highlight of the news is murder. I hope you don't mind not writing about the two people murdered here tonight? Do you realize how important that is? If this was to leak out. Everyone will find out soon enough. You understand, we can't be too careful.

Go ahead and write about Dr. Fine's book and demonstration like you planned to do. Dr. Fine should get some publicity out of this. When I have more to tell you, about the two men that was murdered tonight, I will gather all of you together to get the story first. If you have a little patience, I may have something to tell you soon. After you give Detective Stunning Stephen Edwards the information we need about you, you may leave."

"Uncle Columbo, before Hannibal and me go to follow Jerry, may I suggest some of my thoughts?" asked Scooter.

"Go ahead," replied Uncle Columbo. "Tell just me what's on your mind."

"Is it possible that Dixie and Stephen are also in danger?" suggested Scooter. "Dr. Zodiac may want to kill them next."

"We already know that Dr. Zodiac threatened Stephen and he may be in danger," answered Uncle Columbo. "You may be right about Dixie because of her strange power of her mental skills as a mind reader, she may need police protection. I really think right now we should take Dixie with us to the station. Now that we are done questioning Jerry, we now know that he is taking Dixie back to the hotel to keep an eye on her."

Chapter Nine

MURDER AND MORE

Earlier that day, a strange man living on the same floor as Dixie Doneright and Jerry Dickerson called a maid to his room to put clean sheets on his bed. The maid knocked on the door and the strange man let the maid in.

"Wait," said the strange man, with a creepy look in his eyes as the maid stood in the doorway to his bedroom. "Don't be afraid. There is no reason to be afraid," said the strange man as he approached the maid with a bouquet of flowers in his hand.

"Those are for me?" questioned the maid as she smelled the flowers hearing a popping noise. "Why are they for me? Oh I suddenly don't feel so good."

"Here, have a cigarette," offered the strange man. "Maybe this will make you feel better."

The maid then grabbed a cigarette from the strange man and put it in her mouth. Then the maid lit the cigarette and took a puff and fell on the floor dead. The strange man then took the hotel keys from the maid and put the maid's body in the closet by the front door of his apartment.

As 7:00 p. m. approaches, the strange man is very much aware that Jerry Dickerson and Dixie are both at Dr. Fine's demonstration. Because he knows it's safe, he goes out in the hallway first to Jerry's room and then to Dixie's room, checking out the hotel keys for each room to see if he can get in.

It is now 11:00 p. m. and Dixie is now back in her room at the hotel sound asleep. As she is sleeping, she feels somebody shaking her arm and saying in a hideous voice,

"Wake up Dixie. Wake up Dixie. I am Dr. Zodiac. Your pushing me around and we're not married. If you tell the police anything about me, you won't be pushing, you will be shoving. Then there will be death in your immediate future."

As Dixie opened her eyes, she saw a man standing above her wearing a turbine, a mask of a zombie and a white sheet over his head and body and she began to scream. As she was screaming, the man ran from her room and disappeared. Hearing Dixie scream, Jerry and his gang immediately rushed to her room.

As Jerry entered Dixie's apartment, he began to yell, "Dixie, what happened? Are you alright?"

Dixie began to cry as she answered Jerry, "Don't leave me alone. There was a man who barged in here, standing over me while I was sleeping quite peacefully. He was wearing a turbine, a mask of a zombie and a sheet over his head and body. He said his name was Dr. Zodiac and if I said anything to the police about him, he would kill me."

"Come on. Come on Dixie, pull yourself together," replied Jerry in a comforting voice as Jerry's gang stood behind Jerry eating their Tutti-fruttis. "Come on you Tutti-fruttis," yelled Jerry. "Ace, Lefty, Danny, Shorty, Mugs, go after Dr. Zodiac. Don't let him escape. He can't be too far away. We need to catch him and turn him over to Mr. Detective Stephen to get me off the hook of murder.

We'll show Detective Stephen a thing or two. Next there is only one thing to do, call the police station to have them send Rex, Stephen and Columbo over right away."

Thirty minutes later, Stephen and Columbo was at the hotel knocking on Dixie's door.

"Open up. Come on. Open up this door," demanded Stephen as he again repeated, "Open up. Open this door."

"Somebody is trying to break into the apartment. Boys, let's turn the lights out and get behind the door. Dixie, get in the bathroom and lock the door," instructed Jerry. "I've got a feeling it might be Dr. Zodiac coming back to do Dixie in."

"After the lights were out, Stephen and Columbo barged through the door and was tackled to the floor by Jerry and his men.

"There's two of them!" yelled Ace "And we've got both of them. They're not going to get out of here. Turn the lights on Lefty and let's see who we've got."

"Well, well, if it isn't Stephen and Columbo. This is a surprise," laughed Jerry. "Are we glad to see you. We've been waiting here to talk to you."

"That's a fine way to greet officers of the law," shouted Columbo. "We ought to run you in."

"Take it easy," requested Jerry as Ace and Lefty helped Columbo and Stephen get up off the floor. "We're sorry for tackling you to the floor. We thought you was Dr. Zodiac."

"There is no excuse for what you did," exclaimed Stephen. "You knew we were coming."

"How was we to know you wasn't Dr. Zodiac returning to Dixie's apartment? All you did was knock on the door and then you just barged in," exclaimed Jerry. "You're the ones who should be arrested, because you didn't identify yourselves."

"I'm sorry Jerry. We should have identified ourselves. You can't make a bust on the police," answered Stephen.

"Stephen, you may be great at boxing, but I think you would make a terrible wrestler," laughed Jerry. "Instead of boxing Ace, maybe you might want to get into the ring and have a wrestling match with him."

"Boxing, wrestling, I'll take on Ace either way. I guess we were both in the wrong the way Columbo and I came through the door and you boys tackled us to the floor," explained Stephen. "Columbo and I thought there was something suspicious going on in here. That's why we decided to break in when nobody answered the door."

"I guess we were both trying to be careful, because we didn't know what was going on behind the other side of the door," insisted Jerry.

"Exactly, I guess that makes sense," replied Stephen. "OK, what kind of a story do you have to tell us this time? I love to hear you talk. You make your arguments so plausible."

"Something terrible has happened. Dr. Zodiac was here in Dixie's bedroom while she was sound asleep," Jerry began to say. "He woke Dixie up and threatened to kill her, if she said anything about him to the police. That's why he came here."

"Is that what Dixie said? That's a likely story," answered Stephen. "How long did it take you to dream up that story after you left Dr. Fine's Office? Aren't you overdoing it? Just where is this Dr. Zodiac now? Where did he go? Do you have any idea where he went?"

"Are you kidding? Why would we make up a story like that? He was really here," cried Dixie. "The boys was doing your job and went out to look for him and Dr. Zodiac disappeared into thin air."

"Do you think that's being fair to Dixie?" asked Jerry. "We have a lagitament reason to believe that Dixie's life is at stake. What if he starts popping? He will find her and commit murder. I called you for your help and we need your help before he commits another murder. If anything happens to that girl, I will hold you responsible. It's your job and you have to find him. He's the one your looking for. Don't you see? He wants Dixie out of the way."

"I really saw him. He was wearing a turbine, the mask of a zombie and a white sheet over his head and body. He even had a spooky action at a distance," said Dixie as she began to cry. "He threatened to kill me. I don't want to die. I'm really scared and I need your protection."

"I'm sorry to hear about that," replied Columbo. "I'm sorry if he frightened you. I don't think you have anything to worry now, because everything will be OK."

"Dr. Zodiac took it on the lamb. My boys chased him down the hall and he just disappeared," added Jerry. "We didn't see anything. There was not a sign of him anywhere. He may have gone down the elevator."

"Don't forget, I can read minds," Dixie said as she reminded Stephen and Columbo of her mental skills. "Right now, I know what your thinking and I don't have to be hypnotized to read your mind. You're still doing things halfway."

"What do you mean?" asked Stephen.

"I'm not going to stand for that. You don't believe us and you refuse to help us. That's exactly what I mean. Where is Rex?" asked Dixie.

"He's on his way. He should be here any minute," answered, Columbo.

"Just what will it take for you to believe us?" asked Dixie. "For me to die at the hands of Dr. Zodiac. I was hoping you would help me. If Rex was here, he would believe me."

"I don't blame you. I see exactly how you feel. OK Dixie, when Rex gets here, you can tell him what happened and then well check out your story," replied Columbo. "Our job is to protect and serve. If Dr. Zodiac is some unknown person to you and Jerry, we'll find out. I don't want to waste our time with Jerry if there is a killer on the loose."

"Are you sure you'll help me?" asked Dixie. "I don't want you to check out my story. I told you what you need to know. Now it's your job to find him before it's too late."

"I'm sorry, you seem to be in an awful mess. I'll give you my word that I will do my best to find Dr. Zodiac and arrest him. That's the best I can do," promised Columbo. "You have to understand that every one that was in Dr. Fine's Office is a suspect. We have to check every lead and any ideas that we have that will lead us to the killer. We want everybody who lives in Davenport to be safe. You better keep that window locked. You don't have to worry because Jerry will protect and care of you. We have to leave."

"You can't leave after what's happened," replied a frightened Dixie. "Dr. Zodiac is still on the loose."

"Yes, of course. I would say that you have nothing to worry about. I will take care of it and attend to it myself. You will be safe," explained Columbo.

"What do you mean, nothing to worry about? What are you, a class A cop?" replied a puzzled Dixie. "Don't ask anymore questions. Just do what I say. I don't want to take any more chances."

"I'm not worried about you, Dixie. You know your stuff. As I said before, Jerry and his boys will protect you," answered Columbo. I will also assign a police officer to be outside your door. I'm terribly sorry, but we have to go.

I'm sure that Rex is coming up the elevator now. We will meet up with Rex and tell him what happened. You can always call us if you need us. Stephen, in the meantime, I want all suspicious characters turned in to Rex and me. They are being sought for questioning."

"Dixie, let them go," reasoned Ace. "If they are against staying here, it may be OK. Now it's our job to protect you."

"Well, they're gone," Jerry went on to say. "Dixie, Why don't you stay at my place tonight? If Dr. Zodiac comes back, he won't know where you went. Ace, Lefty, Danny, Shorty, and Mugs, would all of you stay here at Dixie's apartment tonight?"

"I don't think Dr. Zodiac will be back," replied Lefty. "I really hope he does. If he does, this will be our chance to nab him. Then Ace, Mugs, Shorty, Danny and myself can play football with him, by using our fists to pass him around the apartment to each other."

"Dixie, get your things together and come back to my room with me. I think it's time to hit the hay," insisted Jerry.

"I would love to," replied a tired Dixie.

Chapter Ten

THE DEAD CHAMBER MAID

A couple minutes later, Dixie went with Jerry back to his apartment.

"Dixie, you can sleep in my bed tonight. I'll sleep on the couch," offered Jerry. "Let me go into the bed room and make sure the windows are locked."

As Jerry turned on the lights, he jumped back. A dead chamber maid was laying in his bed. A sign was laying next to her that said, "Out Of Order."

"Dixie, don't go in there," ordered Jerry.

"Now what's wrong?" asked Dixie.

"There is a dead chamber maid laying on my bed," explained Jerry. "Quick, call a cop! We have a dead dame on our hands. Wait! I'll call a cop!"

"Oh no, what else can go wrong?" cried Dixie.

"Dixie, you sit there on the couch," requested Jerry in a comforting voice. "I better call the desk clerk of the hotel to see if they can stop Rex, Stephen and Columbo from leaving the hotel.

Hello, this is room 5025. Three Detectives, T. J. Columbo, Rex Tarillo and Stunning Stephen Edwards just went down the elevator," explained Jerry. "Would you stop them and send them to room 5025, immediately?"

A few minutes later, Rex, Stephen and Columbo was knocking on Jerry's door.

"OK Jerry, open up and let us in," ordered Stephen. "And no funny business this time."

"Hold your horses and save your knuckles. It's open. Come on in," answered Jerry in a very serious voice.

"Well, well, we meet again." said Stephen as he entered Jerry's apartment. "What's going on here? Did you send for the three of us?"

"It's a small world," laughed Jerry. "What, me send for you? I never send for anybody, even if I need them."

"Hey, this apartment isn't bad, not bad at all. It looks like an apartment on Park Avenue," exclaimed Stephen. "What was it you wanted to talk to us about?"

"Oh, it was nothing really important. The reason I called you up to my apartment is to show you the main attraction. Now that you are finally here, I have something to show you in my bedroom," Jerry went on to say.

"After Dixie and I left her apartment and we came to mine, I found a chamber maid dead on my bed. I didn't let Dixie in the bed room because I didn't want her to see the dead body. Now I'll have to take Dixie back to her apartment where Ace and the boys are staying in the hopes that Dr. Zodiac will return."

Rushing to see the body, Stephen quickly turned and ran into Jerry tripping him to the floor.

"Get out of my way, Jerry," demanded Stephen. "I want to see the body."

"Hey, I live here you know. You have no right to come in my apartment and trip me!" shouted Jerry.

"Then stay out of my way or I'll do it every time!" boomed Stephen.

"Stephen, I never seen you do that before. Your not sick, are you?" asked Columbo.

"Let's bury the hatchet," pleaded Jerry.

"I would love to," replied Stephen. "Look Columbo, there is a body on Jerry's bed just as he was telling us."

"Guess who this is?" asked Jerry. "I sure don't know who she is."

"You mean to tell me that you don't know a thing about a dead chamber maid laying on your bed?" answered Stephen.

"How should I know? I never associate with corpses," answered Jerry.

"This isn't a guessing game. This is murder," answered Stephen. "How are you going to explain this? Where did this sign "out of order" come from?"

"Somebody set it next to the very dead corpse laying on my bed," explained Jerry.

"Columbo, did you call the ambulance yet?" asked Stephen.

"Sure I did," replied Columbo. "What did you think I was doing on my cell phone, testing it to see if it worked?"

"This could have happened anywhere," replied Jerry.

"But it didn't. It happened here. I can see what happened," reasoned Stephen.

"It looks like that I'm in a very important predicament,"reasoned Jerry. "I have reason to believe that Dr. Zodiac is responsible for this. If you don't find him, I could go back to prison for a crime I didn't commit."

"You still are in a predicament," answered Stephen. "A murder was committed in your apartment. Why do you go around knocking off strangers? It seems like you freaks are running amok. Somebody ought to feed you more often.

Stop shaking your head. I'm not going to spend the whole night here. I may not have caught you in the act, but at last I caught you with the goods and that's what I'm after. I have been waiting for this moment for years."

"Please believe me. I'm telling the truth," pleaded Jerry.

"I don't like being inquisitive, but I don't like working in the dark. I could use a bit of the truth," answered Stephen. "You thrive on this sort of excitement, don't you?"

"We'll, it's better than vegetating," replied Jerry.

"Why can't anyone ever make you live a like other people do?" asked Stephen.

"You mean a normal life with a social security number, a house with a white picket fence around it with a bank book,?" answered Jerry.

"Not anyone?" questioned Stephen.

"Not even me?" asked Dixie.

"I love you very much Dixie. I would do anything for you. When I say anything, I mean I would fight bad guys for you and even kill a dragon or two, but I would not vacuum or wash the dishes. Because of this it is very difficult for me to say, but, uh, I feel in my heart that I am not worthy of you," reasoned Jerry.

"I feel the same way," insisted Stephen.

"Dixie, you would probably want to wait up every night for me, with a light showing through the window," answered Jerry. "I'm not in the habit of going into a house until all the lights are out. Dixie, you're a good looking girl. You would make somebody a good wife."

"I would like to get married if the right man came along," responded Dixie.

"Even if the wrong man comes along, you better grab him," jested Jerry. "Beggars can't be choosers."

"Now Jerry, it looks like I have a legitimate reason to make a good arrest. I'm going to take you to the station and book you myself," promised Stephen. "We need to put you away for safe keeping. With Dr. Zodiac around, you might end up in some bad company."

"Sorry pal. Even though you have a head like a crystal ball, that doesn't prove that I did it. Well, what grips me is that you sound like the same old Stunning Stephen Edwards I knew before I went to prison," boomed Jerry.

"I haven't got time to argue with you. I think there is something fishy going on around here. As I always say, all the foxes always end up at the fur store. First I found you standing over a dead body at the scene of a crime at Dr. Fine's earlier tonight. Now I find you at another one right now," as Jerry and Stephen ranted on at the same time, using the same words.

"Don't you get tired of that routine?" asked Jerry. "I do. Don't you get enough of cops and robbers? Your so bright. It's a waste of time going to Florida. I can get my suntan just sitting next to you. I'm going to give you my finger prints just to prove to you that I didn't kill anybody."

"Bla, bla, bla. You're not going to gab your way out of this one. All of your alibis have the habit of disappearing like a hole in water. Do you want me to give you the last line? I think we have the evidence we need to take you to jail. It's funny, but I don't feel bad about that at all. Your marching down to the jail with me right now. Come on. We better go now.

It is very clear to me that you're sneaking around here. This time I've got you where I want you. It seems that murder is a new hobby with you. You're Dr. Zodiac or the culprit involved in these homicides. Maybe you're covering up for somebody. This time, I should get a promotion. From now on, it's going to be Lieutenant Edwards or maybe even Captain Edwards."

"Wait a minute General. It isn't as simple as all of that. Here we are again, being questioned by an almost human bloodhound, Stephen Edwards. What are you trying to do, dig up that old feud you had with me to get me lynched?" demanded Jerry. "Isn't this getting boring to you?"

"No, I rather enjoy it," answered Stephen. "It's no time to go soft. I have to handle this my own way. To do my job right, it's my job to get the facts. For once my suspicion is justified."

"Stephen, would you listen to Jerry?" insisted Dixie. "You're all wrong about Jerry. You've got to believe him."

"Ain't she wonderful?" beamed Jerry.

"I've got no right to believe him. I know you're in love with Jerry and you trust him," answered Stephen. "He's a pretty swell guy for a heel."

"It doesn't make any sense why they don't use you in the bureau of philosophy instead of homicide, because it's a mystery to the police department," reckoned Jerry. "It would help you in the department if you did something smart. No, I guess I shouldn't said that. I'm fresh out of cigarettes. Would either one of you like a cigar? Those lousy cigars you smoke are ruining your wind."

"I don't mind if I do," replied Columbo.

"Jerry, do you need some money to buy some more cigarettes?" asked Dixie.

"No. I'm loaded. I have a whole two bucks left. You know that I don't smoke cigarettes or cigars myself. They are very bad for your health," answered Jerry.

"Exactly, I totally get that," replied Dixie.

"So how are you going to explain it now that you've been caught murdering people? How do you figure to get out of this one?" inquired Stephen.

"You can't pin the murder of those men at Dr. Fine's on me," Jerry went on to say. "Your not putting anything over on me. You're pretty sure you have something on me, but it's not in the cards. You're loosing your grip by holding a grudge. There were several people at the crime scene at Dr. Fine's. After the lights went out, anybody there could have killed those two men. It really could have happened that way.

Now look, I can explain. I didn't do anything illegal here. I never committed a crime of violence even though you may think I had the urge. After me and my boys left my apartment tonight and went to Dixie's apartment, somebody planted the chamber maid on my bed to make me look responsible for killing her. Why would I have you come to my apartment, if I was responsible for killing her? I wouldn't even bring Dixie to my apartment if I knew there was a dead body on my bed."

"What was you doing here? Waiting for a street car or is it the Miami Special? Save your phony explanation. I presume that if this was for money, it would be money you stole. Nobody could convince me that somebody tried to black mail you and that's why you did this," explained Rex.

"I don't know. Do you care to make me an offer? What am I offered?" laughed Jerry. "If some clown handed me 170 bucks without a gun, think what that would get me. Sure I want the dough, but it's my tough luck, because I know I'm not going to get it. I wouldn't know what to do with it if I got it."

"You could give it to me. I sure would know what to do with it," laughed Dixie. "Do you see what I see? Look on the floor. There is the heel marks of the chamber maid on the carpet. Let's see where they go."

"That sounds reasonable. You may have something there," reasoned Stephen.

"It looks like the heel marks are coming from the living room and right out in the hall," observed Rex.

"Come on. Let's find out if they will lead us to the killer," boomed Jerry. "I don't want to be accused of any murder. Dixie, you stay here."

"Not on your life," screamed Dixie. "You're not going to leave me alone in this apartment."

Everybody then began to follow the heel marks out in the hall way, leading to the elevator. After following the heel marks in the hall way for twenty five feet, they stopped.

"Jerry, you may think that I'm a dumb cop, but I'm not going to ask you any questions," promised Columbo. "Stephen, I want you to close the door and lock it to Jerry's apartment. I want you to stand guard and don't let anybody in. I don't want to loose that body. I'm going to call the an ambulance to come and get the body. Next I'm going to take Jerry to the station and book him, now that we finally have the evidence that Jerry committed a murder."

As Columbo left with Jerry, Stephen locked the door to Jerry's apartment thinking that the dead maid was the only one in the apartment.

The window to the bedroom apartment began to open and in climbed the strange man. The strange man walked over to the dead maid. He picked her up and dragged her over to the window. The strange man climbed back through the window on to the ledge and pulled the dead maid through. Then he disappeared with the dead maid.

Ten minutes later the paramedics arrived at Jerry's apartment.

"We're here to pick up a dead body," explained one of the paramedics.

Stephen then unlocked the apartment door. "Follow me to the bedroom," instructed Stephen. "There is a dead maid found laying on the bed, who has stopped breathing permanently."

"What bed?" asked the paramedic as he looked through the doorway of the bedroom.

"There is only one bed in here," answered Stephen as he pointed to the bed. "That bed right there."

"Did you get us down here to play a joke on us?" asked the paramedic.

Looking at the bed, Stephen yelled, "She's gone! The chamber maid is gone! How can that be? The door to the apartment was locked and I was standing guard!"

"If the dead chamber maid returns, give us a call. We have to go," laughed the paramedic.

Stephen immediately called Columbo on his cell phone and told Columbo about the missing body.

The headlines in the local paper read the next day;

"Jerry Dickerson Arrested For Murder. Police Unable To Find Victim's Body."

"We finally capture a murderer and can't prove he murdered anyone. It looks like you're in the clear for this murder," explained Columbo to Jerry. "There have been three people murdered, with you present at all of them. Then there was the wrestler that was found dead on this very hotel roof that you live in. How do you explain that?

"Are you trying to flatter me into a confession?" asked Jerry. "What you really want to know is how I made the chamber maid's body disappeared. We'll I tell you how I do it. I just snap my fingers like that and the body disappears."

"You're cute, very cute. That's very clever. Suspicion is always the father of truth," added Stephen.

"Your a lot farther from the truth than you think," laughed Jerry.

"It's very interesting watching a great criminologist at work. All I did was walk up to the bodies after they were dead," replied Jerry. "I don't care what it looks like, I didn't kill anybody and I don't know who did. I didn't have anything to do with the dead wrestler on the roof.

You three might even find the real killer if you stop wasting your time trying to prove I'm the killer. I was in prison once and lost the quality of free air. I don't want to go back for murders I didn't commit. You're the Detectives so detect and leave me alone."

"You're our main suspect. You had your big chance and you're not going to get out of this," insisted Columbo. "I don't want you to actually think I cleared you of this murder. I saw the body on your bed with my own eyes. That's why I'm making you the main attraction. I don't know who else would do this. For all I know, you could have had your mind snap as you woke up one morning and began to think killing is a lot of fun."

"Well let me tell you something," Jerry went on to say. "After the first man was murdered at Dr. Fine's Office, Rex told me and my boys that he thinks Detective Murphy is living in this very hotel. He said that Detective Murphy's mind really did snap and he was convicted of two brutal murders."

"That's right. He escaped from the court house," insisted Rex. "He is now a master criminal and is believed to have his face changed."

"Well, there you go. That makes more sense to find him and to quit harassing me for murders I didn't commit," explained Jerry. "It looks like it may have taken another killing to prove my point."

"This time I believe you're serious." reasoned Columbo.

"Exactly, if you don't mind, I'm going take Dixie back to her apartment and I'm going to stay with her," Jerry went on to say. "If you have the time and haven't anything better to do, you may want to look around my apartment and check for clues. You may need a little time to figure things out. Here's the keys to my apartment. Lock up when your done."

"Go ahead Jerry. See if you can make it through the next twenty four hours without finding any more dead bodies." instructed Stephen.

"Don't worry Stephen," replied Jerry. "If I do, you'll be the first person I call."

Chapter Eleven
Dr. Zodiac Visits Margret

That same night, the three detectives began checking out clues of the disappearance of the dead chamber maid at Jerry's apartment, Margret is at home in Northwest Davenport fast asleep. As she is sleeping, she feels somebody poking at her arm and saying in a hideous voice, "Wake up. Wake up Margret. It's Dr. Zodiac. Tell your husband to quit looking for me or I will be back to kill you."

As Margret opened her eyes, she saw a man standing over her wearing a turbine, a mask of a zombie and a white sheet over his head and body. At that moment, Margret began to scream and then she passed out.

Ten minutes Margret began to open her eyes. She looked around the dark room and Dr. Zodiac was gone. Feeling it was safe enough, Margret got up out of bed and turned the lights on. Margret then reached for her cell phone and called Rex on his cell phone.

After Rex picked up his cell phone and answered the call, he realized it was Margret calling.

"Rex," said Margret as she began to cry. "Dr. Zodiac was here while I was fast asleep. He woke me up and said for you to stop looking for him or he would kill me."

"I'm going to call the station and have them send the closest squad car to the house right away. Then I will head right home," reassured Rex. "Please don't talk anymore. Just do what I say. Look for that spare revolver I have in the house. Turn all the lights on and then lock yourself in the bathroom until a police officer arrives.

Stephen, Columbo, keep looking in Jerry's apartment for clues of the missing chamber maid. I have something very urgent to do. I'm sorry if I have to run out on you. Margret is in trouble and I have to go home. When Margret is in trouble, she's in trouble. Dr. Zodiac visited Margret just now while she was asleep the same way he did with Dixie."

Five minutes later, a police officer was knocking on the bathroom window as instructed by Rex.

"Open up the front door Mrs. Tarrillo. This is Officer Norris."

Margret then rushed out of the bathroom to the front door.

"Am I glad to see you," said Margret as she began to cry. "There was this man here. He woke me up and threatened to kill me."

"I know. I know," replied Officer Norris. "Now that I'm here, your going to be safe. While we are waiting for your husband, why don't you make a pot of coffee? It will settle your nerves."

As Margret was sitting at the kitchen table, sipping on her coffee, Rex appeared in the kitchen doorway.

As Margret looked up at Rex, she got up from the table and walked over to Rex and began to cry all over again.

"Now, now, Margret, your going to be OK now that I'm here," promised Rex. "Now tell me exactly what happened."

As Margret began to tell her story to her husband, it turned out to be the same story that Dixie told Stephen and Columbo.

"Now I am going after Dr. Zodiac," vowed Rex. "When I catch him, he is going to wish he was never born."

"But what about me?" asked Margret. "If you do that, he will be coming after me."

"Just keep cool Margret. You will have plenty of protection," explained Rex. "I don't want anything to happen to you, because I can't live without you. Tomorrow, I'm going to hire The West Side Kid's Detection Agency. There are ten of them to look after you. As you know, there is Hannibal, the leader and Scooter. The other eight members are, Who, What, I Don't Know, Because, Smiley, You Don't Say, I'm Not Sure and Whatever."

"But what about Scooter? Nothing doing. You know I can't stand being around Scooter," explained Margret.

"I know dear. It should only be a few days. Right now we don't have enough police officers to watch you night and day. Besides Scooter will protect you," answered Rex. "Wouldn't it be funny if Scooter was alone on the job and Dr. Zodiac came back to the house. Within minutes Scooter would somehow get Dr. Zodiac to drink his chemicals that would make him become a forty inch small fry. Can you picture Dr. Zodiac with short arms and walking around on short legs?"

Thinking about what her husband said, Margret began to laugh.

"Scooter has done some dumb things to us," said Margret as she continued to laugh. "I think it would be good therapy for me to see that Dr. Zodiac turned into a little weasel."

"That's my girl," said Rex as he laughed with Margret. "Officer Norris, I need you to stay the night and keep watch. Margret and I are going to bed."

As Rex began to get ready to go to bed, he opened the door to the bedroom closet and a crazy look came over his face. Inside the closet, leaning against the wall was the missing dead chamber maid. Rex immediately shut the closet door without saying anything to Margret.

Rex then turned around and said to Margret, "After thinking things over, I want you to go in the kitchen and have another cup of coffee. I want to get Officer Norris back in the house, because I need to talk to him."

As Margret went into the kitchen, Rex went out the front door to get Officer Norris. Ten minutes later, Rex went into the kitchen while Officer Norris remained in the bedroom.

"Margret," Rex began to say calmly. "I called Columbo and we talked this over about what happened tonight. I want you to get your things together. I'm going to take you over to stay with Columbo and his wife Janet for a few days. I think you will be a lot safer staying with them."

Chapter Twelve
JERRY DID IT

It is finally eight o clock the next morning and Jerry is beginning to wake up. Thinking to himself, he said, "I better check on Dixie to see if she is OK."

Jerry walked over to Dixie's bed room and knocked on the closed door.

"She's not in there, boss," informed Lefty. "She left five minutes ago and is on her way to Dr. Fine's Office."

"Quick boys, Dixie may be in danger!" boomed Jerry. "Let's get after her right now!"

At that moment, everybody rushed out of Dixie's Apartment.

"Ace, Lefty, Danny, you take the elevator and meet us out in the parking lot," instructed Jerry. "Shorty and Mugs, follow me down the stairs."

Just as Jerry and his men went through the hotel door and out in the parking lot, they saw two masked men trying to push Dixie in a car.

"Hey, Don't do that! Let her alone!" yelled Ace at the two men.

The two men immediately dropped Dixie on the pavement, got in their car and drove away.

Jerry then ran towards Dixie and helped her stand up.

"Dixie, Are you alright?" asked Jerry.

"No I'm not," said Dixie, as she began to cry.

Putting his arms around Dixie, Jerry observed a laceration on Dixie's head and informing Dixie, Jerry said, "Dixie, you're hurt. When you was pushed on the pavement, you hit you're head. You have a laceration on your forehead. I want to find out how bad you're hurt. Can you tell me what day of the week this is?"

"It's Wednesday," answered Dixie.

"Are you sure it's Wednesday?" asked Jerry.

"It looks like a Wednesday," reasoned Dixie.

"I better get you to a doctor," insisted Jerry. "Do you know who those men were?"

"I think I recognized their voices," cried Dixie. "My guess would be that it was Charlie, The Chill and Smitty, The Grim Reaper."

"On second thought, would you boys take Dixie to the ER?" requested Jerry. "Ace, I need you to come with me to look for those two creeps."

"I'm right with you Jerry. I want to get my hands on those varmints," vowed Ace.

It was now 9:15 a. m. one hour later, Smitty and Charlie was unlocking the door to their apartment. Once inside, out from their bedroom walked Jerry and Ace. The door to the hallway was not completely shut.

"What are you doing in our apartment?" asked Smitty. "Who let you in?"

"It's a military secret. This is a charming little place you have here. As if you didn't know why we're here," suggested Ace. "What was you trying to do, give Dixie a free ride about an hour ago?"

"Say what? Just what's going on here? What do you mean, give Dixie a free ride?" asked Charlie. "Just what are you talking about?"

"You know exactly what I'm talking about," replied Ace. "You tried to get rough with Dixie by trying to shove Dixie in your car. Dixie said that you and Smitty are the two bit crooks that had the moxie to do this. When I yelled at you, you shoved her to the pavement and drove away like two bad little boys."

"Why would we do that to Dixie?" asked Charlie. "I thought we were partners."

"Big deal, partner. Plenty big. I think you two need a lesson you won't forget," exclaimed Jerry. "I disapprove of what your saying and I think it's time to play information please. Don't play dumb with us. I want you to tell us anything we ask. If pressure is what you want, pressure is what you're going to get.

Turn around and push your hands to the ceiling. It's a good thing we brought some rope with us because we are going to tie you up like a couple of mummies. I got this idea from you Charlie, because this is an old trick of yours."

"What is this? A double cross?" insisted Charlie.

"In spades," replied Ace. "Jerry told you to turn around. Now do it!"

"You're a little mixed up. You can't prove that was us, because we had masks on," admitted Smitty.

"Smitty, you big dummy. You've done stupid things in the ring when you were boxing. I just can't believe what you just said," roared Charlie as a shot rung out from the hall.

"Smitty's been shot!" yelled Charlie as he saw Smitty fall to the floor. "Jerry, one of your boys did this. I'm calling the police."

"Let's call an ambulance first and get him to the hospital," demanded Jerry.

"Then I think we better call the police station and ask for Detective Columbo and his laughable sidekick, Mr. Stunning Stephen to come right away," exclaimed Ace. "We need to find the killer soon, because after he is found, I want to get The World Middle Weight Chump in the ring. He better warn his muscles, because I am really looking forward to knocking his lights out."

After the paramedics were called, Ace asked Jerry, "Who do I call next?"

"Call the police station and ask for Stephen and Columbo while I keep an eye on Charlie," instructed Jerry. "I'm not going to let Charlie out of my sight."

Ace then called the police station and his call was directed to Rex's Office where Columbo, Stephen, Hannibal and Scooter was discussing the murders at Dr. Fine's Office.

"This is Ace," said the caller. "Can I speak to Detective Columbo?"

"Answering the phone, Rex informing the caller said, "This is Detective Tarillo. Just a minute and I will hand the phone to Detective Columbo."

"This is Detective Columbo. Can I help you?"

"This is Ace, one of Jerry Dickerson's men. Jerry and I are at Charlie, The Chills and Smitty The Grim Reaper's Apartment at Jerry's Hotel. Can you come right away to apartment 6015? Smitty has been shot. I think he's dead."

"We're on our way!" yelled Columbo as he hung up the phone.

"How do you like that? He hung up on me," stated Ace.

"Come on boys. We have to go see you know who at you know where. He is now involved in a shooting," announced Columbo.

"Uncle Columbo, who is you know who and you know where?" asked Hannibal. "Do you want Scooter and myself to go with you? Hmm."

"Were going to see Jerry at his hotel. I know you would like to come along and straighten everything out. Alright, alright, your invited. You better come along before you burst a blood vessel. You can come if you can keep up with us," answered Uncle Columbo.

"Come on Scooter. Wake up. We're going with Uncle Columbo!" shouted Hannibal.

"I'm coming," yawned Scooter.

"Never mind. Just hurry up," demanded Hannibal.

As the paramedics was entering Charlie and Smitty's apartment, the Detectives was getting off the elevator walking toward the apartment.

While Rex, Columbo, Stephen, Hannibal and Scooter entered the apartment, Jerry greeted them saying, "Well come in. You brought quit a crowd with you. I hope the room is large enough."

Rex replied, "This hotel is a busy little place. Tell me exactly what happened. Who is that on the floor and is he dead?"

"His name is Smitty, The Grim Reaper and his days are up," replied one of the paramedics. "His death was due to a gunshot wound to the neck."

"Look everybody. The body is moving," said an excited Scooter.

"Are you sure?" asked Hannibal.

"Sure I'm sure. What do you think, I'm not sure?" objected Scooter. "It looks like post mortus reflex."

"When a dead body moves, it's called rigor mortus," remarked Hannibal. "Boy is that stuff is corny."

"How stupid of me," replies Scooter. "I think so too even though I don't get it. I thought it had to do with whiskey and aspirin."

"Columbo, call the station and have them send somebody up from the lab," requested Rex. "OK Jerry, here we are again with you at the scene of another murder. What's your story this time? I bet it's going to be a whopper. Let's make this short and sweet. We already know the whole story."

"If you know what I did, you tell me," Jerry went on to say.

"I might just do that. I wish I could think of a snappy answer, but you're going to start out with, you're not very good at explaining things, but you didn't kill Smitty," Rex began to say. "Don't be giving me the fast shuffle. If you are reasonable, I'll be generous to you."

"Jerry had it in for Smitty and me," broke in Charlie. "Jerry is a two bit crook who would double cross himself twice a day. He is the torpedo who shot Smitty while he was standing here talking to both of us. Jerry and Ace climbed through the bed room window and was here in our apartment as a reception committee waiting for us to come home."

"How did you climb through the window?" asked Rex. "This apartment is six stories up."

"Jerry and I walked down to the end of the hall where there is a window," explained Ace. "We opened up the window and climbed on a ledge that is about three feet wide. We just followed the ledge around to this apartment. We opened up the bed room window to this apartment and the next thing you know, were in."

"When we got here, Jerry thought Smitty was trying to pull a fast one on him. He just sneered at Smitty and Smitty told him that he was a double crosser and was leaving him holding the bag. Jerry wanted Smitty to take a powder and to get out of town," Charlie continued to say."And that's when Jerry killed my best friend."

"Why you! It was a nice try. Jerry didn't say anything of the sort. That's one of the oldest gags in the world. This will kill you. Jerry never said anything about that," boomed Ace. "Jerry wouldn't kill anybody. What are you trying to put over on us? You're not going to try and kid us?"

"You're sure not going to kid me," answered Stephen. "Ace, just who do you think you are?"

"You know who I am," replied Ace. "I'm Jerry's right hand man."

"That's not what he calls you," roared Stephen. "What kind of stunt are you trying to pull? It's getting to look like Jerry is a suspicious character who can't start or end his day without killing someone, There is really not a dull moment with him. Now he is really in a jam. I guess Jerry doesn't know the seriousness of this."

"Don't make me laugh! Your the crazy one! You can't tie me into this! You don't even know what you're saying!" screamed Jerry. "You could be wrong. I think you will feel terrible when you find out that I'm on the level. You can't pin the rap on me. Are you going to believe that? For once in your life, would you believe that I am telling the truth?"

"Well, I guess we've got this case sewed up," remarked Scooter. "It's all in a day's work."

"What have you done to help?" asked Hannibal.

"I'm here, aren't I?" reasoned Scooter.

"What do you bet?" answered Hannibal.

"What are we going to do with Charlie?" asked a puzzled Scooter.

"Why don't you call a cop," laughed Hannibal. "If you really want to give us a hand, shut up."

"OK Uncle Columbo, why don't you take over from here?" reasoned Scooter.

"Thanks for your help Scooter. You have been a mighty big help in this case," answered Uncle Columbo.

"You must be crazy. That's a lie. I can explain everything. Jerry couldn't have shot Smitty. He even didn't have a fire cracker," protested Ace. "The door to the hall way of this apartment was partially opened. I don't know who did this. Somebody shot Smitty and clipped him through the door."

"That's a likely story. Are you quit sure your telling me the truth? I'm no good at riddles," reasoned Columbo.

"Jerry, did you hear that? Columbo just said a terrible thing to you, insisted Ace. "He just called you a liar."

"I know. He really knows how to hurt a guy," answered Jerry.

"Quit your stalling. Don't you think its strange that you are always at the scene of a murder?" asked Columbo. "Who's on you're list to kill next?"

"Will you quit saying that? I don't know what you're talking about. Am I under arrest?" asked Jerry.

"What do you think? I'm sorry. It looks like I have to put you under arrest," explained Columbo. "It's just a mere technicality. I want to talk to you some more at the station."

"Is that news or propaganda?" questioned Jerry. "Are you sure you have the right guy?"

"I'm going to make sure," promised Columbo. "I'm not only accusing you of murder. There are a lot of other charges against you. One of them is felony."

"One thing I resent is that you're putting us to a lot of trouble to prove you are guilty of murder," exclaimed Stephen.

"You're really a wonder, because you are putting Jerry to a lot of trouble to prove he's innocent. You think you have an open and shut case. You can't get away with that!" yelled Ace.

"Well, I'm doing it," roared Columbo.

"Don't forget, I get one free call to my lawyer," insisted Jerry. "If you can show me how he was murdered, then you will have me. May I sit down?"

"Please do. Your not going to wiggle your way out of this one. It looks like your out of luck," reasoned Columbo.

"I don't know anything about anything," replied Jerry. "I just came up here for a ride on the merry-go-round."

"Wait, I have a jolly good idea. There are a couple of formalities I want to check out. So I can do this, the three of you stand in the same spot when Smitty was shot. Now show us where Smitty was standing. Ace, if what you're saying is true, Smitty would have been shot from behind," exclaimed Stephen as he turned to talk to the paramedics. "Show us where the bullet entered Smitty's body. Make sure you know and tell me every detail."

The paramedics looked at Smitty's neck and explained that the bullet was lodged in the back of Smitty's neck.

Stephen then announced to everyone, "Jerry couldn't have killed Smitty, because the bullet is in the back of Smitty's neck. Jerry and Ace was standing in front of Smitty."

"Stephen, thanks for helping us prove our story," Ace went on to say. "You don't miss much, do you? It looks like you saved Jerry's life. Here's to the best cop in the world. Now when I get you in the ring, I won't hit you as hard as I planned."

"That is quit OK," replied Stephen. "To show you my appreciation, I won't knock you out in the first round."

"Ace, how would you like to get in the ring with me again and box me?" asked Scooter. "I'm not afraid of you, because I know I can beat you."

"There is no way I'm going to box you. Stephen will be in the ring invisible again. I won't be boxing you. I will be boxing an invisible Stephen," exclaimed Ace. "Did Stephen put you up to this? That's the only way Stephen can box me and win."

"Stephen didn't put Scooter up to this, you chicken," replied Hannibal. "This is just an excuse so you don't have to box Scooter. Your loosing your nerve and your afraid to box Scooter, because with the skills I have, I will be his manager and you be sure to loose."

"You and Scooter don't have any skills in boxing," laughed Ace. "Scooter, if you was to go in the ring without Stephen, just how are you planning to beat me?"

"I will knock you out just like I did in Stephen's dream," explained Scooter.

"Your going to do what?" asked Ace. "Just what are you talking about?"

"In Stephen's dream, I started to shiver all over when I faced you," answered Scooter as he was hiding behind Stephen. "You was so frightened, you couldn't move and I knocked you out."

"Then how about you and me have our fight here and now?" roared Ace. "Show me how you knocked me out in Stephen's dream. Even though Stephen is here, I can see him. He won't interfere because he will be scared stiff to fight me."

"Ace, your on. After this is all over, I will be looking forward to meeting you in the ring! I will be visible and you will find out how scared I am of you. You won't see the punch coming that will knock you out," bragged Stephen.

"Now to move on in this murder investigation, my next question to you Charlie is, why did you accuse Jerry of killing Smitty when you knew he wasn't responsible?"

"I'll answer that for Charlie," offered Jerry. "This morning out in the hotel's parking lot, me and the boys saw Charlie and Smitty trying to force Dixie in their car. Ace yelled at them to let her go and they pushed her on to the cement and drove away. My boys took Dixie to the ER because she hit her head on the cement and injured her forehead.

Ace came up to this apartment with me to confront Smitty and Charlie about trying to kidnap her. We thought one of them might be Dr. Zodiac because of what happened last night with Dixie. As we were talking, somebody from the hall way shot Smitty."

"What about that Charlie?" asked Stephen. "Are one of you Dr. Zodiac? Is that why you went to Dixie's apartment last night, to scare her and threaten her not to tell us about you?"

"No, not neither one of us is Dr. Zodiac," answered Charlie. "Smitty and me was just playing a joke on Dixie. We didn't mean to hurt her. It looks like Smitty paid the ultimate price for trying to pull a joke on Dixie. Now I lost my best friend."

"You still didn't answer my question. Why did you accuse Jerry of killing Smitty when you knew it wasn't true?" repeated Stephen.

"Before Jerry and his gang went to jail, they chased Smitty and me clear out of Davenport," explained Charlie. "I guess I lost it with my best friend dead. Because of that, I thought this was the perfect time to get even with them for Smitty and me."

"Jerry, do you want to press charges against Charlie for accusing you of murdering Smitty?" asked Rex.

"No I don't," replied Jerry. "What I do want is for Charlie to stay away from Dixie."

"If he bothers her again, he will have to deal with me," exclaimed Ace. "After I'm through with him, he will want to leave Davenport permanently. Maybe on a stretcher."

"I wouldn't do that Ace. Remember, you're still on parole," scolded Columbo.

"OK, I will remember that as long as you do your job and keep Charlie away from Dixie," roared Ace. "Dixie is already frightened by Dr. Zodiac. She don't need this creep bothering her,"

"What about that?" asked Rex. "Are you going to leave Dixie alone or do I have to take you to jail?"

"My best friend Smitty is dead and I don't need any more problems by going to jail, so I will leave Dixie alone," replied Charlie.

"See that you do or I will personally arrest you," promised Rex. "OK gang, let's move on to Jerry's apartment. I ran into another problem last night and I need to talk to all of you in private."

"What do you want to talk to me about?" asked Jerry. "I never committed a crime of violence or even had the urge to. Are you still trying to pin the murder rap on me?"

"No Jerry. It's something you Columbo and I all have in common," insisted Rex. "I don't want to say any more until we get to your apartment."

"OK Rex. As curious as I am, I'll wait," exclaimed a puzzled Jerry.

Chapter Thirteen
THE LETTER

A few minutes later, Jerry was opening the door to his apartment as the gang waited to go in. Now the gang is in Jerry's Apartment and the door is shut.

"What's that on the floor?" asked Scooter as he bent down to pick up an envelope.

"Give that to me," ordered Hannibal as he grabbed the envelope out of Scooter's hand. "This envelope is addressed to Jerry. Here Jerry, take this envelope."

Looking at the envelope, Jerry remarked, "I never seen this envelope before. Somebody must have shoved it under the door."

"Well open it up," beamed Scooter. "Let's see what it is?"

Jerry then opened up the envelope and pulled out the letter inside. He then began to read the letter.

"To Mr. Jerry Dickerson.

I have a message for all of you.

This is a warning. You ask, who am I? You will soon find out that I am a Mysterious Scorpio. A seething heinous villain who has a score to settle with each of you. You might also call me a secretive ghoul who is hell bent on revenge and plotting the demise of all of you. I have deep emotional intensity with blank stares and a deadpan humor. You may also think I'm intrusive and I'm reading your mind.

I will give you one clue. You can find me in a deep dark cave.

My warning to you is as of now, you are all fugitives of an autopsy. I've got a lot of unfinished business to take care of. You thought I was giving you all trouble before. As of now I am including everybody ta get inta da act. Man is the only animal that can be skinned more than once and my plan is to pull all of you apart. Don't ever let Dixie Doneright alone, because this lady will need a hand. As you know, I went to her apartment once for a visit.

My first order of revenge is to make another visit to Dixie. I have given myself a rain check to come back where I will plot to carry out her demise.

My second order of revenge is a plot to carry out your demise, Jerry Dickerson.

My third order of revenge is a plot to carry out is the demise of the stooges that work for you, Ace, Lefty, Danny, Shorty and Mugs.

My fourth order of revenge is a plot to carry out the demise of Detective Stunning Stephen Edwards. Being a World Middle Weight Boxing Champion won't do you any good.

Then my last order of revenge Margret Tarillo, Detective Rex Tarillo's wife and last of all, Detective Columbo and his wife, Janet.

You may ask why I'm doing this? The key word is revenge. Obviously after you read this letter, this is only a waste of today if you think this is your chance for making plans to run away by waiting for tomorrow. It won't do any good for any of you as long as I keep my eyes on all of you, because I will always know where you are. Don't try and stop me or bother looking over your shoulders for me. You won't see me there. Remember, your all mice and I'm a hippopotamus. Mice cannot shadow like a hippopotamus.

I'm not stopping now. I don't care if you believe me or not. You may think I've given you enough of a ride already. When I find you, it will be your tough luck. I have special plans for each of you. Don't bother staying up at night waiting for me. When you do see me, it will be too late. When you do go to sleep, it will be an eternal sleep.

Ha, ha, ha. Have a ghoul day and a restless night.

Dr. Zodiac

After reading the letter, Jerry said to everyone, "Wow, this is breaking the camel's back. This letter is more important than anything you have on me. After all of you came into my apartment, I thought I was in trouble again. After reading this letter, it say's we're all in trouble. I will show you this letter, then you will have to make a deal with me."

"Say what? Just what's going on here? What's so important about that letter?" asked Stephen.

"I'm certainly glad your all here to see this letter. This is a letter of horror from Dr. Zodiac and according to this letter, we're all in a jam," cried Jerry. "This letter says he is planning the demise of all of us here, plus Dixie and your wives."

"Give me that letter to read," requested Columbo.

After reading the letter, Columbo said to Stephen and Rex, "Now we really have problems. This letter is quit extreme but very effective. It looks like Dr. Zodiac is trying to stretch all of us like strings on a banjo. Then he is planning to play a beautiful tune on us. You better let me read this to both of you."

After reading the letter out loud, Columbo then said, "Now both Jerry's and my finger prints along with Dr. Zodiac's are on the letter. I'm going to put the letter in the envelope very careful. Does anybody have a clean handkerchief I can use to wrap around the envelope? We need to check both of them for fingerprints. It may be too late, because Jerry's fingerprints are also on the letter and envelope. I will still take them to the lab to have them checked out."

"I made a deal with the three of you and I'm going to hold you to it," demanded Jerry.

"Now you know why we want to talk to you Jerry," explained Rex. "You know what happened last night? Dr. Zodiac visited my wife, Margret while she was sleeping. I wish I had been there to face Dr. Zodiac. What you don't know at this time, to my horror is I found the missing dead chambermaid. Your the last person I wanted to tell after chasing you down as the killer. That's why I had to leave our little meeting last night, to go home."

"What do you mean? Just where did you find the chamber maid?" asked Jerry.

"This is a little embarrassing," exclaimed Rex. "Because you were standing over dead bodies, you was being accused of murder. The press doesn't know about this and Margret doesn't either. If I tell you, will you keep this to yourself. If Margret or the girls find out, it will really scare them. Dr. Zodiac has now visited Dixie and Margret. Columbo, I think your wife, Janet is next."

"OK, I think I can keep my mouth zipped shut," promised Jerry. "Let's have it Detective. Where did you find the dead chambermaid?"

"After I went home to Margret and she told me of Dr. Zordiac's visit, I finally calmed her down," explained Rex. "I was starting to get ready for bed and opened up the closet door to the bedroom and I about threw up. The chamber maid was leaning on the wall inside the closet. I quickly shut the door and took Margret to Janet and Columbo's house."

"Since you found a dead body in your closet, you should be arrested for murder," laughed Jerry. "That's a likely story. What are you hiding? Don't tell me what I can see with my own eyes. How long did it take you to dream that one up?"

"I know. I know. I deserved what you just said," insisted Rex. "You took those words right out of my hat."

"How are we going to protect the girls with this killer on the loose?" asked Jerry.

"My plan was to hire The West Side Kids Detective Agency to protect Margret," explained Rex. "If you want to bring Dixie to my house, she should be safe."

"I have a better idea. With the way everything is coming together, with the letter, it's a different ball game. Since Margret is already staying at my house, why don't everyone come to my house? That includes you Stephen and your gang Jerry," insisted Columbo. "You know Janet and I won the lottery a couple years ago. We bought a house by Emise Park that has 5,500 square feet. It's on three acres and big enough for every one. It has a very good security system. We also have two German Shepherds. What do you think?

Hannibal, would you and your gang be interested in coming?"

"Uncle Columbo, you don't have to ask me twice," promised Hannibal. "If it wasn't for you sending us all to The University of Davenport, we would never have our Detective Agency. Besides, you and Janet are family. We'll be ready for Dr. Zodiac if he comes."

"Jerry, do you and your gang want to come?" asked Columbo.

"We sure do," replied Ace. "I really want to get my hands on Dr. Zodiac, but Dixie's safety comes first. If we all band together, all three girls will be safe."

"OK Jerry, let's meet at Emise Park in the parking area close to Locust Street by the dental office in about two hours," instructed Rex. "One of us will come and get you from there. I'm going to call Margret and tell her we're going to be guests at the Columbo's for a few days."

"I'm going to call Janet and tell her about having company," remarked Columbo. "Won't she be surprised about having a house full of guests?"

"I hope she thinks it's a good surprise," added Rex.

"Janet is a good wife," reasoned Columbo. "She won't mind a bit. Our house is very big for two people. She would like having the company.

Hannibal, you know where I live. Get your gang together and come as soon as you can. What are you waiting for?"

"I'm on it," replied Hannibal. "Come on Scooter. Head em up and move em out."

"I'm not going to tell Margret anything about why we're all going to your house. It will really scare her," replied Rex.

"I don't think I'm going to tell Janet anything," replied Columbo. "When we get everyone together, then we can sit down and talk about it."

"Come to think of it, I'm not going to tell Dixie anything," Jerry went on to say. "When we are all together, the girls will feel safe when we tell them what is going on. I'm not even going to tell my gang about this letter I got from Dr. Zodiac. They can also find out about the letter once we're together. I'm leaving now. I'll be at Emise Park in two hours."

Chapter Fourteen
The Retreat To Columbo's House

It was now 1:00 p. m. at the Columbo's house. The girls had just finished preparing lunch. The counter tops was filled full of food. Card tables was put up with chairs surrounding the tables.

"Come and get it!" yelled Janet. "This is self serve. Grab a plate and dish up!"

Everybody filled their plates full of food and sat down to eat as if this was a family gathering.

As everybody was eating, Scooter said to everybody, "When my mother has to make dinner for several people, she makes twice as much as she needs and then only serves half. When she wants to make a ham, she puts a large ham and a small ham into the oven. When the small ham burns, the large ham is done."

"I never thought of that," replied Janet. "I have to try it."

"Janet, do you think I should have children after thirty five?" asked Dixie.

"I can answer that," explained Scooter. "I don't think so. Thirty five children is enough for any woman."

An hour later, every one was finished eating and all the leftovers was put in the refrigerator.

"Now that we're done eating, let's adjourn to the family room," instructed Columbo.

After everybody was seated in the family room, Columbo stood up in front of everybody to talk.

"Rex, Stephen, Jerry and I have a very serious matter to talk to all of you about," Columbo began to say. "Some of you may wonder why we're all here together with Jerry Dickerson and his gang after Rex, Stephen and myself tried to pin a murder rap on poor Jerry here. I hardly know where to begin. What I have to say concerns all of us."

"How can that be?" remarked Lefty. "What kind of thing would affect all of us?"

"Columbo wants to start up a football team and have the girls be our cheerleaders," replied Scooter in a serious voice.

"I think I would really like that," beamed Margret. "With my mental problems I have, that would really help me feel better. I still would like to be hypnotized by Dr. Fine."

"Maybe I could arrange to have Dr. Fine do that for free," insisted Dixie.

"That's out of the question," ordered Rex. "The decision is not yours. As of now, you girls are not to leave the house."

"Hey, what's going on here? You can't do that. Look, what is this all about?" asked Margret. "I want to know the whole story. Why is it a problem that I can't see Dr. Fine or leave the house?"

"I'll say it in two words," explained Rex. "Dr. Zodiac."

"Oh him. You have to be flexible. What are you sitting around here for? Why don't you hurry up and catch him so I can get hypnotized by Dr. Fine?" questioned Margret.

"We're working on a plan to catch him," answered Rex. "Right now, our first priority is to keep you girls safe. An envelope with a letter inside from Dr. Zodiac was shoved under Jerry's door of his apartment. I think it's time to pass it around for everyone to read and understand how much danger we are all in and when I say all, that includes Columbo, Stephen and myself."

"Uncle Columbo, does that mean we're not going to have a football team with cheerleaders?" asked Scooter.

"I'm afraid not," answered Uncle Columbo. "We're going to form our own team with a defense and attack strategy against Dr. Zodiac.

If you promise to be a good boy, my first order of business is to make you an Honorary Police Detective. How would you like that?"

"If you're really going to make me a Detective, you bet I will like it. Will I be just like you?" questioned Scooter.

"That's absolutely right. Only you're going to be a special kind of Detective. Your going to be like a secret service agent. Except for everybody here, you're not to tell anybody that you're a Detective. Your first order of business will be protecting the girls at all costs from Dr. Zodiac," explained Uncle Columbo.

"I hope Dr. Zodiac shows up here. Just wait until I get my hands on him. I will break both of his arms and both of his legs. Next I will give him a dirty look," assured Scooter.

"I already feel better with Scooter on the job," added Margret. "You don't happen to have any extra chemicals around to give Dr. Zodiac something to drink?"

"What do you mean?" asked Scooter.

"You know. The mixture that turns people into a forty inch small fry," answered Margret.

"I have my chemicals at home. Do you want me to go home and get them?" offered Scooter.

"Yes," answered Margret. "Girls, I'm going to feel safer with Scooter on the job. Don't you agree?"

"I sure do. I'm going to feel safer with a strong man on the job," reasoned Aunt Janet.

"Hannibal, I'm going to make you Scooter's Assistant. Take care of Scooter. We need him. Would you take Detective Scooter home to get his chemicals?" asked Uncle Columbo. "When you come back, make sure nobody is following you. Now that Scooter is on the job, the rest of us can work on our plans."

"I understand," replied Hannibal. "I will get the job done."

"Now that I'm your boss, you better do what I say or else," vowed Scooter.

"OK boss. Get in the car so we can go get your chemicals." teased Hannibal.

"OK Chief, let's get going before I report you to Uncle Columbo," roared Scooter.

"Now that Scooter is gone, I want to tell everybody that I am really scared," exclaimed Margret. "I didn't realize that Dr. Zodiac had it in for all of us. So this is what he's after. What are we all going to do?"

"It can't be all that bad," said a puzzled Janet.

"Janet, I guess you really don't understand the predicament we're all in," added Dixie. "You haven't had Dr. Zodiac come to your bedroom while you was asleep and wake you up with his hideous voice. That happened to me and I was really scared."

"Dixie, you don't have to worry about that anymore," explained Rex. "Come on. The marines are here to stay. You might say that we're at a fort with plenty of soldiers to protect you."

"That's right," reasoned Janet. "We have an amazing security system and two German Shepard for protection with a built in police protection. We never will have to call the police, because they are right here."

"I know how that works," replied Jerry. "Once that bloodhound, Stephen Edwards gets on your trail, he never gives up. I was afraid for a while if I didn't find Dr. Zodiac, I would be convicted of a murder I didn't commit."

"OK Jerry, so I was doing my job by being on your trail," remarked Stephen.

"You do that so well," laughed Jerry.

"At least you have been eliminated as a suspect of these murders. For a while, it didn't look good for you," reasoned Stephen. "Now that we're all in this together, maybe we can find this Dr. Zodiac and get him arrested for all these murders."

"I tried to tell you that I didn't commit any murders. You just wouldn't listen to me. A man who is trailed by the police most of his life soon becomes a Detective, himself," answered Jerry. "When this is over, Ace still wants to box you. I would like to find out how if it's possible for me to be a real Detective."

"What?" answered Ace. "You want to be one of those blood hounds?"

"I sure do. Now that I'm out of jail, I would like to find a respectable job," Jerry went on to say. "Stephen, if you can be a Detective, why can't I?"

"When this is over with, I will let you talk to the captain about this," promised Columbo. "With the right training, I think you would make a great Detective."

"I also think so," added Stephen. "When this is over with, I am anxious to continue to box."

"Rex, what happens now? Do you and Columbo have any ideas what we're going to do next?" asked Stephen.

"To begin with, with Jerry and his crew, there are six men. The West Side Detective Agency gives us ten more men. With Stephen, Columbo and me adds up to three more, making a combination of twenty men."

"You're wrong," reasoned Hannibal. "That makes nineteen of us, not twenty."

"OK, there's nineteen of us," answered Rex. "There is still enough of us at the fort to protect the girls. Jerry and his crew and The West Side Kids are to stay here at the house and watch over the girls. They are to not leave the house for any reason.

If we need groceries, four of us are to go to the store with Janet and stay together. Stephen, Columbo and myself will work on finding Dr. Zodiac. He thinks we're just ordinary cops with no imagination. I, myself would like figure out how to catch him in a punch line mouse trap.

Keep your cell phones with you at all times. If any of us run into trouble, call for help. Tomorrow, I think Columbo, Stephen and myself should go down to the hotel and search all the rooms for Dr. Zodiac."

"I'm in this as deep as the rest of you. Can I go with you?" asked Jerry. "Stephen and I have always been at odds. Maybe we can team up and find Dr. Zodiac together. I have a score to settle with Dr. Zodiac for scaring Dixie."

"Stephen, it's your call. Do you want to work with Jerry?" questioned Rex.

"I want to catch this moron like everybody else," replied Stephen. "Jerry, if you don't loss your cool and remember that I'm the boss and that you will do everything I say, then we can work together."

"If I can work with you that will help me get started as a Detective, I can do that," answered Jerry.

"That's good, answered Rex. "Now we can work as two teams. Columbo, what do you say?"

"That's fine with me partner," agreed Columbo. "Just to be on the safe side, I think we should have two uniformed officers with each of us. We may be the hunters, but we're also the targets."

As the men continued to talk, Hannibal and Scooter returned with Scooter's chemistry set.

"Hello boys," greeted Uncle Columbo. "Scooter, I see you brought your chemistry set with you. What is that other thing you have in your hand?"

"This is my ant colony," replied Scooter. "My philosophy is that if you can love ants, you can love anything. If I'm going to be away from home for a while, I thought I should at least bring my ants to keep me company with my chemicals."

"Scooter, your amazing. You think of everything," laughed Uncle Columbo.

"I just need to know what room is mine so I can put my ants and chemicals in there," reasoned Scooter. "I don't want anything to happen to my chemicals or my little friends."

"Janet and the girls are busy now fixing us all something to eat that is self serve, so I can't ask her right now," explained Uncle Columbo. "I think your bedroom is on the lower level facing the back yard."

"Thanks Uncle Columbo. I'm going to take my little friends down there right now, before something happens to them," insisted Scooter as he turned and left for the lower level of the house.

Twenty minutes later as everybody was in the kitchen putting their favorite foods on their plates, a loud scream was heard from the lower level of the house. Everybody dropped their plates.

"Who's missing from our group?" asked Columbo.

"It's Ace!" yelled Jerry. "Dr. Zodiac is here and Ace is in trouble!"

"Rex, Stephen, grab your pistols. The rest of you stay here and guard the girls," instructed Columbo. "We need to go to the lower level of the house as fast and safe as possible to rescue Ace."

As the three men entered the lower level, Ace came out of his bedroom shouting and scratching.

"Are you OK?" asked Columbo. "What is all the racket and commotion about? We thought Dr. Zodiac was down here with you."

"Ants, ants, they are everywhere," replied Ace as he slapped one of his check. "I came out of the shower and got dressed. Ants are in my clothes and in my bed. They're everywhere."

As Ace was talking about the ants, Scooter started downstairs.

"What are you doing with my ants?" asked Scooter. "You leave them alone. They are mine and I want you to quite trying to hurt my little fellows."

"So it was you. You're the one responsible for this," boomed Ace as he slapped an ant off of his arm. "I might of known it was you. I should be slapping you around, instead of these ants."

"Temper, temper!" yelled Scooter. "Leave my little friends alone!"

"Don't you even think of hurting my buddy," demanded Stephen. "If you try it, you won't have to wait to get in the ring with me. We'll have it out right here and now. When I'm done with you. You will think that your going through ten rounds with The World Heavy Weight Boxing Champion, Joe Lewis, blind folded with your hands tied behind your back."

"Uncle Columbo, don't let Ace hurt my ants!" screamed Scooter.

"Boys, knock it off right here and now. Stephen, your suppose to be a Professional Detective. You above all should know better than to behave that way," scolded Columbo. "We may be living together for quit some time. We need to work together to get out of this mess. Ace, try to find some clothes that are ant free. I'll get Hannibal and The West Side Kids to come down and catch these little creatures."

"Thanks Uncle Columbo for helping me save my ants," said a grateful Scooter.

"Columbo, I'm sorry I said that to Ace," said a guilty Stephen as he put out his hand to shake hands with Ace. "Ace, instead of fighting, let's be friends. If I find Dr. Zodiac, I want you at my side to help me give him a few bruises. Just be glad that you had to deal with Scooter's ants instead of drinking his chemicals."

"Why, what's the difference? Soap and water can never change the perfume of a skunk. If it is connected to Scooter, it always means trouble," exclaimed Ace.

"We all know that," replied Columbo. "Rex found that out when Scooter was in his chemistry class."

"That's because I'm always doing something stupid," explained Scooter. "I don't mean to, but I'm always doing dumb things like having the lid off of my ant colony. I not only made you mad, but you hurt my ants and I'm sorry."

"I'm sorry I got mad at you Scooter," said a puzzled Ace. "What happened in Rex's Chemistry Class?"

"Well it's like this," explained Columbo. "A couple of years ago, I paid for the tuition for Scooter and The West Side Kids to go to The University Of Davenport. Rex made a batch of chemicals to drink, to help him control his temper. When Scooter was in his class, he made a batch of chemicals as a class project. Scooter somehow switched his chemicals with Rex's. Scooter continued to add chemicals to Rex's Chemicals and made a bomb out of it. He threw the bomb out the window into the parking lot. It landed on Rex's new car and blew it up.

Later that day, Rex drank Scooter's Chemicals and shrank down to a forty inch small fry. Rex began to commit crimes and as a police officer, it was my job to catch him. After I caught Rex and he went to court, the judge gave Rex a choice to go to jail or work with me as a Detective."

"You have to understand that Scooter means well and has a heart of gold," added Stephen. "I think we all learn from a hen to never boast about an egg until it's hatched. When you get to know Scooter, you will feel the same way about him, as the rest of us."

"Scooter, I'm sorry I got mad at you. I guess I lost my mind for a hot minute. It is kind of funny now that I think about it," laughed Ace.

"That's why when I went home to get my chemicals, I just had to bring my ants along as company," explained Scooter. "The reason I went home to get my chemicals was to make a batch of chemicals for Dr. Zodiac to drink and make him a forty inch Zombie."

"You go ahead and make those chemicals," insisted Ace. "When we catch this Dr. Zodiac, I'm going to jam those chemicals right down his throat. Then we'll see how horrifying or scary a forty inch Dr. Zodiac can be?"

"His size isn't going to make any difference," explained Columbo. "When Rex was forty inches, he was very deceiving with the crimes he committed and was very hard to catch. Just as Scooter was responsible for Rex's size, Scooter was also responsible for Rex's capture."

"All my troubles began with Scooter," Rex began to say. "When I was younger, I was a captain in the navy. Next I taught chemistry at The University Of Davenport. Then along came Scooter, well meaning Scooter. Then within the first hour of my class, he began to destroy my life little by little. And to put a play on words, that's when I became little with short stubby arms and legs. I was getting to be known as Little Rex and I turned to a life of crime all because of the stupid things Scooter did to me.

It turned out for the better, because now I'm working with Columbo as a Detective. I also ended up marrying my girlfriend, Margret. I had family issues with my brothers and sister. Scooter was also the reason I was caught by Columbo who is now my best friend.

When you understand Scooter, you can't help but like him. His mind is like a cover on a book. The cover seldom tells the truth about whats in the book. To find the truth, you have to read the book. He is like a glass that is half empty or half full. His mind is like a parachute that was designed to have only one function after it's opened.

Scooter is also the reason I took Margret to see Dr. Fine. She has trouble sleeping and other issues, because of what she went though with me as a small fry. That's why she wanted Dr. Fine to hypnotize her, because nobody else can help her. I guess you can say that's why we're all together today, because of Scooter.

It started out that Scooter was Hannibal's buddy who always tried to protect Scooter since they were kids. Now he is a buddy to all of us. Now Scooter and The West Side Kids are like family to all of us."

"Now that I understand you Scooter will you forgive me for the way I have been treating you?" asked Ace.

"You bet I will," answered Scooter. "I thought that life was harder because I was always saying and doing stupid things. Because my mind works so fast, when I think of something to say I do something stupid because I say things before I even think of it. I always thought it was just a curse. It turns out that this curse has made me a lot of friends who are like family to me."

"Well then friend, I want to be considered one of your family members. Come on Scooter. let's get working on those chemicals for a special take out order for Dr. Zodiac. I think we should name these chemicals, Scooter's Revenge," suggested Ace. "This is something I want to personally deliver to him. I want to see if Dr. Zodiac will do something stupid by drinking your chemicals."

"If it has anything to do with Scooter, he will do just that," replied Rex. "Dr. Zodiac is no match for Scooter, because Scooter is our secret weapon with his ingratiating humor. That's why Columbo made Scooter an Honorary Police Detective. By the way, I have a special badge to give you Scooter to make you a Detective."

"Thank you Rex. Thank you Uncle Columbo," said a grateful Scooter. "What are my orders?"

"I want you to be in your room, where you can work on your chemicals without anybody bothering you," explained Uncle Columbo. "You sit and work on your special chemicals. These chemicals are not to leave this room until I'm ready for them. I don't want anybody drinking your chemicals by mistake. Do you understand?"

"I sure do," answered Scooter. "You are all my family and I don't want to do something stupid with my chemicals."

"Uncle Columbo, since you made me Scooter's Assistant, I will keep an eye on Scooter and his chemicals," promised Hannibal.

"OK, that takes care of one of our plans to take care of Dr. Zodiac," stated Uncle Columbo.

"I just thought of something," reasoned Hannibal. "All we talk about is Dr. Zodiac, Dr. Zodiac. None of us has ever talked to him or even seen him. We don't even know what he looks like. I sometimes wonder if he is a real person."

Hannibal, I'm surprised at you," scolded Rex. "Dixie and Margret has seen and talked to Dr. Zodiac. If you were to ask Dixie or Margret if he was a real person, They would give you an ear full. Because of their mental state, it's best that you don't talk to them about Dr. Zodiac. Do you understand?"

"I'm sorry, I forgot about that," insisted Hannibal. "Because it's all talk, he doesn't seem real to me."

"You and The West Side Kids just stay at the house and protect the girls. He's real alright and maybe you won't have to meet this horrifying killer," answered Rex.

"Stephen, if Jerry is going with you to look for this Dr. Zodiac, I want to take up that offer to go with you," offered Ace.

"Are you sure you want to join the hunt for this Dr. Zodiac?" asked Stephen. "I have to look for this creep because this is my job. I don't want anything to happen to you and Jerry."

"You're darn too tin I do," answered Ace. "If I'm going to be a family member, I want to help out. Dr. Zodiac has been doing all the killings and Jerry has been getting all the blame."

"Then that's settled," exclaimed Columbo. "I think we better spend the rest of the day making plans for defending the girls and Rex's home. Then we better plan for the hunt and begin tomorrow. I think it time to go upstairs and join the girls and make our plans."

As the men returned upstairs Janet asked, "What the big emergency was downstairs?"

"Ants," replied Rex. "Scooter's ants. It turns out that somehow the lid to the ant colony came loose and all the ants got into Ace's bed and clothes. That's why Ace yelled. Because after he got dressed, ants were all over him and boy was he mad."

"Now I'm fine with what happened," explained Ace. "Columbo and Rex explained to me about Margret's encounter with Scooter and how he messed up Rex's life for a while. He also told me about Margret's problems due to Scooter. I guess the ants makes me part of the club. Margret, if there is anything I can help you with, count me in.

I'm in hopes that if I can get Dr. Zodiac to do something stupid by drinking Scooter's chemicals that will turn him into a forty inch small fry. I really hope this will make you feel better. That's my plans. We're going to call Scooter's chemicals, Scooters Revenge."

"That does make me laugh. Thanks for your concern," replied Margret. "After what Dr. Zodiac did to all of us, I think after he drinks the chemicals, he should never be restored to his original size."

"The food is getting cold. Let's all go eat and forget about this Dr. Zodiac for a while," insisted Janet.

"Right on," exclaimed Ace "Lets eat, talk and get to know each other better like a real family."

Chapter Fifteen
The Hunt Begins

The next morning as everybody was eating breakfast at The Columbo residence, Columbo turned on the television to get the morning news.

"We have a special warning out to the residences in The Quad City Area," the television news anchor began to say. "There have been sighting last night of a hideous man wearing a zombie mask, a turbine and a white sheet over his body. He was seen in northwest Davenport looking in windows scaring home owners. Nobody knows what he was looking for. It appeared he was looking for something or somebody. Stay indoors and keep your windows and doors locked. He is suspected of killing three people here in Davenport. If anyone has any information on this character, You are instructed to call the police immediately."

"Rex, I think better call the station. Then I think we better finish our breakfast and go look for Dr. Zodiac," instructed Columbo. "Everybody knows what their job is."

After the Detectives left Columbo's house, Margret said to Dixie, "Would you get me an appointment to see Dr. Fine? I need to see him right away and I want to get hypnotized today. This is all getting to be too much for me."

"You know what Rex said about you leaving the house," objected Hannibal. "It's too dangerous for you to leave the house. Rex left me here in charge to take good care of you."

"I'll take care of him when I see him. Now will some of you nice boys accompany me to see Dr. Fine," asked Margret. "I really need to go and I'm going. Who's coming with me?"

"If you decide to go against Rex's wishes, I guess because we were hired to protect you, Scooter, me and The West Side Kids are all going with you," insisted Hannibal.

"Dixie, since I'm going to have a big escort, would you call Dr. Fine?' asked Margret.

"I'll call him right away," answered Dixie. "I'm going along in case Dr. Fine needs some help to hypnotize you."

"Lefty, me and The West Side Kids are going to take Margret and Dixie to Dr. Fine's Office against Rex's wishes," explained Hannibal. "Margret insists on going. We were hired to protect her, so we have to go with her. You, Danny, Shorty and Mugs needs to stay behind and protect the fort."

"Rex isn't going to like this one bit," answered Lefty.

"I know he isn't. Margret insists on going and we can't stop her, so we have to go with her," reasoned Hannibal.

While Dixie was making arrangements for Margret to go to Dr. Fine's Office, Hannibal took Scooter aside to talk to him.

"Scooter, this situation is getting very convoluted," whispered Hannibal.

"You're right. It's beginning to look convoluted to me. That's for sure," answered a puzzled Scooter. "I have just one question."

"And just what would that be?" replied Hannibal.

"What is convoluted?" asked Scooter.

"You don't know what convoluted means. I'm surprised at you. Dr. Zodiac is making everything convoluted which is messy, tricky," explained Hannibal. "I think Rex and the boys are checking out the apartments right now at the hotel where Jerry and Dixie live.

Now here's what I want you to do. Grab your mixture of chemicals you made last night and put them in a paper sack. When we get downtown, I don't want you to make things convoluted by saying anything to anybody. I just want you to quietly leave and go to the hotel and look for Rex. When you find him, tell him about Margret going to Dr. Fine's Office."

"I'm an Honorary Detective and I will get the job done," promised Scooter.

Ten minutes later after the group went out the front door, Scooter looked down and saw Janet working in her flower garden, next to the house.

"Janet, what are you doing on your hands and knees?" asked Scooter.

"I'm looking for weeds," answered Janet.

"Did I hear you right? Did you say you was looking for weeds?" inquired Scooter.

"You heard me right. I'm looking for weeds," replied Janet.

"Why would you be looking for weeds? Nobody likes weeds," reasoned Scooter. "I have a better idea. Everybody like flowers better than weeds. Why don't you look for flowers instead?"

"I don't know what I was thinking," laughed Janet. "Your absolutely right. I'm going to start looking for flowers."

A very red brick laying on the ground by the flower garden. Picking up the brick, Scooter looked at it and immediately fell in love with the brick.

Scooter then asked, "Janet, I found a very nice red brick by your flower garden. Can I have it?"

"Why sure Scooter. You can have it," answered Janet. "What on earth do you want with a brick?"

"This is really a nice red brick. I like real red colors. Do you have a paper sack I can put it in?" asked Scooter.

"Just a minute. I have to go to the kitchen to get you one," replied Janet.

Twenty minutes later, the gang was parked in front of Dr. Fine's Office. As everybody was getting out of the car Hannibal said to Scooter, "Scooter I think you better wait in the car. Margret's going to have Dr. Fine hypnotize her due to you and your chemicals."

Knowing what Hannibal wanted him to do, after every body went into Dr. Fine's Office, Scooter left the group and walked to the hotel.

After he entered the building, he walked up to the desk clerk and asked if he had seen the Detectives.

"Oh, if you want to find the police station. Walk up one block to Fourth Street and go west to Fourth and Harrison," answered the desk clerk.

"I just want to find the Detectives," answered Scooter.

"Now pay attention. If you want to find the Detectives go one blocks up to Fourth Street and then go west to Fourth and Harrison and you will find the Detectives at the police station," repeated the desk clerk.

"I didn't ask you how to find the police station," replied Scooter. "I am looking for the Detectives searching the apartments in this hotel."

"You have some nerve asking for directions for someplace you don't want to go. I've got work to do, so don't bother me again. I don't know about any Detectives that are searching the apartments at this hotel,"scolded the desk clerk as the phone rings and he picks up the phone.

"I'm sorry, you've got the wrong number. So what if you haven't told me who you're calling. No matter who your calling, he just left. You still have the wrong number, because I don't have a telephone. I'm not even here, so call back later."

Scooter thought to himself, "Here I thought I was always doing something stupid. This desk clerk is really coo coo. I'm sure there is a butter fly net out there with his name on it. I'm not going to find out anything from him."

Scooter then decided to look for the Detectives on his own, starting with the second floor and then the third floor. Not finding a trace of The Detectives, he then went to the fourth floor. As he was walking down the hallway on the fourth floor, a man wearing a Zombie Mask, a turbine and a white sheet over his body jumped out of nowhere in front of Scooter.

"I'm Dr. Zodiac," said the man.

Without thinking about it, Scooter reached out his hand to shake and said, "I'm Scooter."

As he did that, the brick he was carrying fell out of his hand right on the foot of Dr. Zodiac.

"Ouch! Ouch!" screamed Dr. Zodiac jumping up and down on one foot in pain and then the other.

"I'm sorry. I didn't mean to do that Bub. I was just trying to be social able," said Scooter. "I'm always doing something stupid and because of that, the brick slipped out of my hand. Just where are my manners?"

"You idiot. You lame brain," screamed Dr. Zodiac still jumping up and down with pain. "Have you been drinking or have I? If I was a character in a movie, then I could say that I can explain everything. I just don't get it. Just what kind of person walks around carrying a brick?"

"How should I know? What's the fuss? I don't see anything wrong with carrying a brick around. It was a nice looking red brick. Janet was nice enough to give it to me before I left the house. She never said anything about me carrying a brick around. Why would she?" explained Scooter. "I'm very sorry if I dropped it on your foot. May I ask who you are Bub?"

"I can't tell you yet and my name is not Bub. My foot is in extreme pain!" yelled Dr. Zodiac jumping up and down. You say your sorry you dropped it on my foot, you idiot!" screamed Dr. Zodiac still jumping up and down.

"If your name is not Bub, you better tell me who you are!" shouted Scooter.

"You don't know who your dealing with. These are the conditions that prevail. I'm Dr. Zodiac, I'm a man of many sides. Besides being a Mysterious Scorpio, a seething heinous villain, I'm a world traveler and a dreamer."

"You don't look like a world traveler or a dreamer to me," reasoned Scooter.

"I'm going to plot your demise right here and now!" screamed Dr. Zodiac. "What's the matter? Am I making you nervous? Are you getting the jitters?"

"Hot cha, cha. Oh pipe down. I don't know what all that means when you use big words like that. Is that a compliment?" asked a puzzled Scooter.

"No, that's not a compliment! I can say what I want!" objected Dr. Zodiac.

"Exactly. That sounds reasonable. I stand corrected. You still have some nerve bothering innocent people," replied Scooter as tried to help make Dr. Zodiac feel better. Forgetting what the chemicals were for, Scooter pulled the jar of chemicals out of his bag. "I've got a better idea. I think this will help, so drink this. This should make you feel a lot better."

Trusting Scooter's judgment, Dr. Zodiac grabbed the jar of chemicals and took the lid off. In desperation, he gulped all the chemicals down to the last drop.

"Now do you feel a lot better," asked a concerned Scooter. "I'm really sorry I dropped the brick on your foot."

"What was that liquid you gave me? Do you have any more? It really tasted good," asked Dr. Zodiac as he began to shrink.

"Ooh, ooh, ulp, I forgot what those chemicals were for. My mistake. I should have known better," answered Scooter.

"Are these chemicals you gave me the same as drugs?" asked Dr. Zodiac. "What does somebody like you know about drugs?"

"A lot," replied Scooter. "When I was a kid, my mother drugged me all over the place. She drugged me with her when she went shopping. She drugged me to school. She even drugged me to ball practice."

Looking at his arms and legs getting smaller and smaller, Dr. Zodiac began to shout, "What's happening to me? Am I getting smaller or is this sheet I have over me getting larger?"

"I hope this doesn't make you mad at me, but can you keep a secret?" asked Scooter.

"Sure I can," replied Dr. Zodiac.

"Good, I'll bring you one," answered Scooter. "Your starting to shrink. That drink I gave you were chemicals that I made. When somebody drinks them, it will turn them into a forty inch small fry."

"You can't do that to me. I am going to warn you. You can't get away with things like that, It's all on you. I'm Dr. Zodiac, a Mysterious Scorpio, a seething heinous villain. Is that clear?"

"Don't be so gruesome," laughed Scooter. "Correction please. That's the wrong overture. You are now shrinking to a forty inch Dr. Zodiac who is a Mysterious Scorpio and a seething villain. I'm sorry this is happening to you."

"I don't know how that can happen. This has gone far enough. I want you to know that I meant what I said! I'll get you for this!" yelled a desperate Dr. Zodiac taking his Zombie mask and turbine off while the sheet he was wearing fell to the floor. He then ran to the elevator on his legs as they became shorter and shorter, running away from Scooter.

Dr. Zodiac climbed into the elevator and pushed the button to go to the hotel lobby.

Scooter ran to the stairs, going down one flight at a time until he reached the lobby. The elevator doors opened up and out ran a forty inch Dr. Zodiac. As he ran past some women talking to the desk clerk, one of the women remarked, "Look at that little guy. Isn't he cute?"

Dr. Zodiac then ran to the stairs, running back up to the fourth floor. Seeing this, Scooter climbed into the elevator and pushed the button for the fourth floor.

As Dr. Zodiac reached the forth floor, he opened up the door to a small room and pushed a button on the wall inside the room, just as Scooter climbed off the elevator. As the elevator doors closed, the floor to the elevator began to open up where you could see the bottom of the elevator shaft.

Still in the small room with the door shut, Dr. Zodiac remained hidden as Scooter walked past down the hall way. Seeing his chance to get away, Dr. Zodiac bolted out of the small room running as fast as his little legs could carry him to the elevator. He reached up to push the button to the elevator and the doors opened. Anxious to get away from Scooter, he ran into the elevator with the floor of the elevator still open and fell to the bottom of the elevator shaft.

Seeing what happened to Dr. Zodiac and not knowing what to do, Scooter reached around the corner of the elevator and hit the button to put the elevator out of service.

"I'm going for help," Scooter said to himself. Next he started running up the steps looking for the Detectives. As he reached the fifth floor, he saw the Detectives standing by the elevator, waiting for it to arrive.

"Don't think of getting on the elevator!" yelled Scooter.

"And why not!" yelled Stephen.

"Don't ask questions. Just hurry and follow me down the steps to the fourth floor," answered Scooter.

"We're coming!" yelled Uncle Columbo. "Lead the way."

A couple minutes later, Scooter and the Detectives was standing in front of the elevator on the fourth floor.

"Watch your step. That's going to be a big one if you get in the elevator, because there is no floor," explained Scooter.

"What happened?" asked Rex.

Scooter then went on to explain about how Margret wanted to go get hypnotized by Dr. Fine, his red brick and Hannibal instructing him to go to the hotel to find Rex. He then went to tell about Dr. Zodiac jumping out in front of him.

"I reached out my hand to shake his hand and dropped my red brick on his foot by accident," explained Scooter. "To make his foot feel better, I forgot what my chemicals were for and gave him the chemicals I had in my sack to drink and he became a forty inch small fry right in front of my nose. He ran away from me taking the elevator to the lobby and I ran down the steps. I took the elevator back here to the fourth floor and he ran up the steps. After I just got out of the elevator and started walking down the hall, Dr. Zodiac ran to the elevator and fell down the elevator shaft."

Rex carefully looked in the open floor of the elevator and down the elevator shaft seeing the small body of Dr. Zodiac.

"It looks like our troubles are over," laughed Rex. "Ace, see what I told you about Scooter. He isn't just lucky. He's the hero of the day, because he is always cooking on the front burner. Dr. Zodiac was no match for Honorary Detective Scooter. He never lets us down. Scooter handled this one alone and he did it again with his chemicals. He turned Dr. Zodiac into a forty inch small fry."

"Ace I'm sorry if I did something stupid again," muttered Scooter. "You really are the one who should be angry about this. I gave Dr. Zodiac my chemicals to drink by mistake. I should have known better, because you said you wanted to be the one to jam those chemicals down his throat. I didn't even have enough sense to jam the chemicals down his throat. I just handed him the jar of chemicals. He took the lid off the jar and just drank the chemicals and then he asked for more."

"You did just fine," laughed Ace. "I wasn't there to give him the chemicals, so you did it for me."

"You mean I did something right?" asked Scooter.

"Your darn toot in," replied Ace. "You are the hero of the day. I think everyone in your adopted family will appreciate what you did."

"All of us was afraid of Dr. Zodiac, because of what he threaten to do to all of us," exclaimed Stephen. "All it took was a red brick and your chemicals to fight back with, to end our problems with Dr. Zodiac. I think the next time I have a boxing match, I'm going to take a nice red brick in the ring with me."

"I agree," laughed Ace. "I think Scooter has shown us a new way to fight. The next time I fight, I'm going to take a nice red brick into the ring with me."

"Now we know how everybody died. Even the dead wrestler on the roof," added Columbo. "He fell through the opened elevator floor to the bottom of the elevator shaft and was then carried up to the roof."

"Correction," replied Rex. "The lab does not know how the chamber maid died. We know that Dr. Zodiac killed her, but now that he is dead, we'll never find out. Scooter, what are you doing in the hotel walking around with a brick? The plan was for everyone to stay at Columbo's house."

"The only one's who are at Columbo's house is Janet and Jerry's friends," replied Scooter.

"Did I hear you right?" asked Rex. "Where is Margret, Dixie and The West Side Kids?"

"After you left, Margret insisted on getting hypnotized by Dr. Fine," explained Scooter. "Dixie called Dr. Fine at Margret's request and made an appointment to go see Dr. Fine. Hannibal said we couldn't stop her from going, so Hannibal and The West Side Kids went along to protect her. Hannibal instructed me to go find you once we reached Dr. Fine's Office. I found this nice red brick outside Columbo's house. Janet said I could have it. Everybody is at Dr. Fine's Office right now."

"Columbo, would you mind finishing up here with Dr. Zodiac in the elevator shaft?" asked Rex. "I need to go find Margret right away."

"I understand," answered Columbo.

"I also want to go to Dr. Fine's Office," offered Stephen.

"Since Dixie is there at Dr. Fine's, I'm going to go," snarled Jerry. "I don't want Dixie going to Dr. Fine's Office anymore."

"I guess we're all going to desert you Columbo. You'll have to call in for extra help," suggested Rex.

"Don't worry about me. Just go, go, go, get out of here," insisted Columbo.

Chapter Sixteen
MARGRET GETS HYPNOTIZED

As Scooter and the Detectives are still at the hotel, talking about Dr. Zodiac and his encounter with Scooter and his brick, Margret is in the process of making arrangements of getting hypnotized.

After Margret, Dixie and The West Side Kids entered Dr. Fine's Office, Hannibal said to The West Side Kids, "We're here to protect Margret and Dixie from Dr. Zodiac. So that we're ready for any kind of trouble, keep your eyes peeled and let's do The Grand Slam Routine if Dr. Zodiac shows up."

"Young man, what's going on here? What's with this Grand Slam Routine?" asked Dr. Fine.

"It's as simple as this," replied Hannibal. "Dr. Zodiac threatened to kill Margret and Dixie while they was sleeping in their bed and we're here to protect them from Dr. Zodiac. He will have to go through the nine of us to get to Margret and Dixie. Margret is here to see you to get hypnotized and Dixie came to help you hypnotize Margret."

"How can I help you dear lady?" asked Dr. Fine. "How is being hypnotized by me going to solve your problem?"

"I have had terrible headaches and have been having trouble sleeping," explained Margret. "I have seen several doctors and none of them can help me."

"Do you have any idea what are causing these problems?" asked Dr. Fine.

"I can say it in one word, Scooter," answered Margret.

"Oh, him. I can't go through with that, because he really embarrassed me when I hypnotized him. Now I'm having trouble sleeping and when I do, I have nightmares," replied Dr. Fine. "Did he come with you? Is he one of these young men. If he's here, I don't think I can help you."

"Scooter is not here. You just have to try and help me. I have been keyed up all day. Between Dr. Zodiac and Scooter, I just can't take it anymore," begged Margret as she pulled five one hundred dollar bills out of her purse.

Looking down at the $500.00 Dr. Fine then offered Margret to get hypnotized.

"I should know this answer. How did you become a victim of this Scooter? I mean to say what did Scooter do to cause you these problems?" asked a puzzled Dr. Fine.

"Now my husband is a Police Detective. Before that he taught chemistry at The University Of Davenport," demurred Margret. "Scooter was in his class. Before the first class was over, Scooter made a bomb out of his chemicals and threw it out the window in the parking lot. It landed on my husband's new car, blowing it up."

"Is that all he did?" questioned Dr. Fine.

"What do you mean, is that all he did?" cried Margret. "We're talking about Scooter. My husband made up some chemicals to drink to help control his temper. Scooter made up some chemicals as a class project. Some how Scooter switched his chemicals with my husband's chemicals. Later that day, my husband drank Scooter's chemicals by mistake and shrank down to a forty inch small fry. Then my husband, Rex turned to a life of crime and I helped him."

"Even though your husband had to deal with this Scooter, he seems normal to me. How can Rex be a Detective if he turned to a life of crime because of this Scooter?" asked a confused Dr. Fine.

"I hate to tell you this part. Scooter has a heart of gold and even though he is always doing something stupid, he means well. He even was responsible for capturing Rex as a small fry," explained Margret. "Rex had a brilliant mind in his criminal activities. The judge gave

Rex a choice to go to jail or to work with Columbo as a Detective. Since then, I have had these head aches and trouble sleeping."

"I'll tell you what," replied Dr. Fine. "I happen to have a special price of $500.00. I'll call it a Scooter Special to hypnotize you and undo in your mind about all this nonsense that Scooter inflicted on you. If it works, I may have to get somebody to hypnotize me for the same reason known as Scooter."

"Do you really think you can help me?" asked an excited Margret. "Just hearing you say that you can undo what Scooter did to me, makes me feel better."

"Just sit over here in this chair by my desk and I will begin to hypnotize you," instructed Dr. Fine. "Dixie, where have you been? Hiding from this Dr. Zodiac."

"That's right," said Dixie. "Dr. Zodiac has turned Margret's life and mine upside down. That's all I can tell you. We're not suppose to be here. When Rex finds out, he's going to be furious. Let's get this over with, so we can leave."

"OK Dixie, give me one of your ear rings for Margret to look at," instructed Dr. Fine. "Margret, look only at Dixie's ear ring," said Dr. Fine as he started to swing in back in fourth in front of Margret's eyes. "You are getting sleepy, very sleepy. All you can hear is the sound of my voice and nothing else. You are in a deep sleep very deep sleep.

We're going back in time where Rex is teaching chemistry at The University Of Davenport. You and Rex are very happy. Do you understand?"

"I understand," repeated Margret. "Rex and I are very happy."

"Repeat what I'm telling you. Scooter was never in Rex's Chemistry Class," Dr. Fine continued to say. "You don't know Scooter. You never meant Scooter. If somebody asks you who is Scooter, you answer that you don't know him."

"Scooter was never in Rex's Chemistry Class," repeated Margret. "I don't know Scooter. I never meant Scooter. If somebody asks me who Scooter is, I answer, I don't know him."

"Your head aches are now gone and you can now sleep at night," continued Dr. Fine.

"My head aches are now gone and now I can sleep at night," Margret repeated.

"After I give you one more treatment, you need to contact Dr. Nejino to continue your treatments. He owns a large home where he has an office east of 6th and Gaines Street on top of the hill. Do you understand?" asked Dr. Fine.

"I understand," answered Margret. "I need to contact Dr. Nejino to continue my treatments. He owns a large home east of 6th and Gaines Street on top of the hill."

"OK Margret, when I snap my fingers you can begin to wake up," instructed Dr. Fine "Margret, do you feel any better?"

"I feel a lot better, better than I have felt in a long time," answered Margret.

"Do you know any Scooter," asked Dr. Fine.

"That name sounds familiar. No, I don't know any Scooter," replied Margret.

"Margret, do you know me?" asked Hannibal.

"What a silly question. Of course I know you," answered Margret as Rex entered Dr. Fine's Office. "Your Hannibal Columbo and you run The West Side Kids Detective Agency. You work with my husband Rex and your Uncle Columbo."

"What did you do to Margret?" asked Rex as he approached Dr. Fine.

"It's Rex," observed Hannibal. "Margret, you go with the boys and wait in the car. I'll try and talk Rex out of boiling you in your own blood."

As Margret stood up to leave for the car, Rex stopped Margret and asked, "Margret, do you have a fifty dollar bill?"

"I'm sorry Rex, I just bought a candy bar and now I'm broke," answered Margret. "It seems like everybody wants money."

"Come on Margret, you've got money to burn. You must have if you can pay Dr. Fine $500.00 to get hypnotized," laughed Rex.

"Why don't you stop laughing at me and act like a Detective! Go find some clues or something!" yelled Margret.

"Now where are you going?" asked Rex.

"Slumming," answered Margret.

"Where?" repeated Rex.

"I'm going to the car. Hannibal is going to stay here and tell you about me getting hypnotized," explained Margret as she left for the car.

"I'll tell you what he did to Margret," insisted Hannibal before Dr. Fine could answer. "He hypnotized Margret for $500.00 and told her that Scooter was never in your class, that she never meant Scooter and she doesn't know him. This is really going to hurt Scooter's feelings, because he really likes Margret. If he thought Margret wasn't his friend any more, I don't think he could handle it. He also told Margret that Dr. Nejino has an office at his home east of 6th and Gaines on top of the hill where he will continue her treatments."

"Margret came to me and begged me to hypnotize her. I only did what Margret paid me to do," explained Dr. Fine. "I didn't have any idea if my hypnotizing Margret worked. The only way for me to find out was to ask Margret. So I asked Margret, how she felt? She said she felt better than she has in a long time. Then I asked her if she knew anybody by the name of Scooter? She answered that she heard that name somewhere before, but she was sure she didn't know any Scooter."

"Then I asked Margret if she knew who I was," explained Hannibal. "She told me that I run The West Side Kids Detective Agency. That I work with her husband, Rex and my Uncle Columbo. Rex, where is Scooter? I sent him over to the hotel to look for you Columbo and Stephen."

"I'm right behind you," announced Scooter. "What's wrong with Margret? Doesn't she like me any more?"

Hannibal, you and the boys take Margret and Dixie back to where we were all staying," instructed Rex.

"Good old Scooter found Dr. Zodiac and solved our problem with him," laughed Stephen. "It looks like this case is solved and I can go back to boxing."

"Don't forget about boxing with me before you leave," remarked Ace. "I want my chance to box you while your here. You gave Jerry and me a bad time over all the murders. Now I want to give you a bad time in the ring."

"Ace, do I get to box you?" asked Scooter.

"I have a better idea. Why don't you help me train to fight Stephen?" suggested Ace.

"Stephen, is that OK if I help Ace," asked Scooter. "I'll learn him how to box real good, but I won't let him hurt you."

"I guess that's alright. Go ahead and help Ace," replied Stephen. "How am I going to beat Ace if you teach him to box?"

"You have to lose sometime. I'm going to learn Ace really good how to win," answered Scooter.

"OK, I think I can stay another week to box before I leave," answered Stephen. "Scooter, you learn Ace really good, then I'm sure he will beat me."

"Dr. Fine, Stephen and I have to go back to the hotel and finish up there. We'll catch up with you later and explain what happened," promised Rex.

Now with Dr. Zodiac's death, is the case closed or is it? Did Dr. Fine really help Margret forget who Scooter is? What will Dr. Nejino's Spooks do for Margret? Will everybody start carrying bricks around with them? Will Scooter start a brick collection? And the most important question of all. Will Scooter learn Ace how to box well enough to beat Stephen or will it become a convoluted boxing match? Read on to find out what happens next beginning in chapter seventeen.

Chapter Seventeen
BRICKS, COINCIDENCES AND MORE CHEMICALS

It is finally 6 p. m. and everybody has dished up a plate of food and sitting around in the kitchen, talking at Columbo's home.

"Now that the day is about over, I think we better talk about what we're going to do next," announced Rex as he stood up before everybody. "As everybody knows by now, Dr. Zodiac is out of our hair, so we can go back to our normal lives. He is as dead as a door nail."

"How did that happen?" asked a puzzled Janet. "Did you smart Detectives catch Dr. Zodiac at the hotel?"

"We tried, but we couldn't find him," answered Stephen.

"Then what happened to him?" quizzed Janet.

"Technically you started the ball rolling," laughed Columbo.

"Now how could I do that? I never left the house," replied a puzzled Janet. "Are you joking with me?"

"It's no joke. You started the process by letting Scooter have one of our bricks," answered Columbo.

"You don't have to say any more. When you talk about Scooter with a brick, I can imagine the rest," laughed Janet.

"Who's this Scooter you're talking about?" asked Margret.

"You know very well who Scooter is," reasoned Janet. "You even told Scooter that you felt safer from Dr. Zodiac now that he was on the job."

"Janet, I've never meant Scooter and you know it," replied Margret. "Are you trying to play a joke on me?"

"Margret, why are you telling everybody that you don't know me?" cried Scooter. "Did I do something stupid and now you hate me?"

"You didn't do anything stupid to Margret," explained Rex. "Right now, she really doesn't know you. I'll tell you later what happened to her."

"Rex, why are you telling this Scooter that," yelled Margret. "You know that I've never seen him before."

"Calm down Margret. Just forget about it for now. I know. We all know that you haven't seen Scooter before," answered Rex. "We're going to talk about Dr. Zodiac Now you're upset and it's better that you don't hear this. Why don't you go in the bedroom and lay down so you will fell better?

Now that Margret has left the room, I want to tell all of you about Scooter and Dr. Zodiac," Rex continued to say. "While we was looking for Dr. Zodiac at the hotel, Hannibal sent Scooter to get us, because Margret went to Dr. Fine's to get hypnotized. When Dr. Fine hypnotized Margret, he told her that when she awoke, that she never meant Scooter and doesn't know who he is. That's why Margret doesn't know who Scooter is. Dr. Fine then referred Margret to Dr. Nejino for further treatment.

After Scooter reached the fourth floor and was walking down the hall way, Dr. Zodiac jumped out in front of Scooter, wearing his Zombie Mask, turbine and sheet. Scooter told us that he put his hand out to shake with Dr. Zodiac's hand and the brick he was carrying slipped out his right hand and landed on Dr. Zodiac's foot. Forgetting what the chemicals do, Scooter offered Dr. Zodiac his chemicals to drink, so he would feel better.

Dr. Zodiac drank the chemicals and shrank to forty inches. Realizing that he was now smaller than Scooter, the race began. Dr. Zodiac ran to the elevator and took it to the lobby to get away from Scooter. Scooter ran down the steps to the lobby to try and catch Dr.

Zodiac. After the elevator stopped at the lobby, Dr. Zodiac ran out of the elevator. Scooter got in the elevator and rode up to the fourth floor while Dr. Zodiac ran up the steps to the fourth floor with a plan. After Scooter got out of the elevator and the doors closed, Dr. Zodiac was in a small room. After Scooter walked past Dr. Zodiac while he was hiding in the small room, he ran to the elevator to get on. When he entered the elevator, the floor was open to the elevator shaft and he fell to his death."

"Here we're all frighted of Dr. Zodiac and he was no match for Scooter. Just how does he do it?" asked Jerry. "I guess we all think Scooter doesn't know anything. Scooter is smarter than we think he is and he saved the day with a brick believe it or not. Now it looks like we're free to move back in our apartments at the hotel. Rex, did you ever find out how the elevator floor opened up?"

"We traced a switch in the small room where Dr. Zodiac was hiding in," explained Rex. "He had to be the one who flipped the switch to open up the floor to the elevator. In the excitement of being chased by Scooter, he forgot the floor was opened when he got into the elevator.

That also explains how the wrestler was killed. He fell through the floor of the elevator. We also believe that the wrestler knew Dr. Zodiac. Dr. Zodiac gave the wrestler instructions to get on the elevator and then flipped the switch to open up the floor of the elevator. Then Dr. Zodiac went to the bottom of the elevator shaft to get the wrestler and he carried him up to the roof. What we don't know is why Dr. Zodiac killed the wrestler or if there was some one else involved."

"Who was Dr. Zodiac?" quizzed Hannibal.

After we checked his finger prints, we found out that it was Detective Murphy," explained Columbo. "Because Jerry and his gang ran him out of the Quad Cities is why he was living in the same hotel as Jerry. He knew that Jerry and his bunch was being released from prison. This was his big chance to get even with Jerry. Now that we are able to connect the dots, it is all starting to make some sense."

"Do you know who killed the chamber maid?" asked Stephen.

"All we know is that some kind of pill exploded in her face, answered Rex. "The pill alone wouldn't harm anyone. Something else combined with the pill killed her. We don't have any idea what that would be. Scooter at least solved our problem with Dr. Zodiac."

"It was all because I did something stupid," Scooter went on to say. "I was just trying to be friendly by shaking hands with Dr. Zodiac when the brick fell out of my hand onto his foot."

"Sure you were just trying to be friendly," laughed Stephen. "We all know how you operate."

"Now that this is over with, tonight we can celebrate with Dr. Zodiac out of our hair forever, because of our hero, Honorary Police Detective Scooter. So why don't all of you stay the night so we can get to know each other better," offered Columbo. "Now we can talk about something other than Dr. Zodiac. Jerry, if you still want to be a Detective, Rex and I will take you down to the station to talk to the captain tomorrow."

"You better start training hard tomorrow Stephen. I know your only going to stay in Davenport for another week so you and me can box," added Ace. "Now that I know how tough Scooter can be, I want him to learn me how to box. When I'm done with you, it will seam like you've been hit in the face with a brick, over and over. After Scooter learns me how to box, when you leave Davenport, be a good fellow and take me with you as your boxing manager?"

"Go ahead and let Scooter learn you how to box," laughed Stephen. "I'm sure Janet has a brick or two she can give me. You won't even stand a chance."

"Stephen, if you and Ace don't stop it, I'm going to hit you both in the head with a brick," laughed Janet.

"Dixie, what can you tell me about this Dr. Nejino?' asked Rex. "He took me aside at Dr. Fine's demonstration and told me he could help Margret. He said he deals in spooks to cure people."

"He goes by two names," explained Dixie. "Michael The Magnificent when he works with Dr. Fine and Dr. Nejino when he works with his spooks. He likes to find women with mental problems and then he's happy-nasty happy and charges them $500.00 a session with his spooks."

"I think we should make him unhappy-nasty unhappy. Does he really help these women?" asked Rex. "It seems like we're dealing with too many doctors. You might say that there is something spooky going on here."

"I've helped at these sessions. They could be plausible. I don't know if these women are really being helped," replied Dixie. "I always thought there was something strange about Dr. Nejino, but I couldn't put my finger on it. I always wondered if he was victimizing these women.

As Michael The Magnificent, he was helping Dr. Fine with his new book, "The Healthy Benefits Of Hypnotism". He didn't like me working with Dr. Fine and I don't know why. I think he hired Charlie The Chill and Smitty The Grim Reaper to keep me from working with Dr. Fine."

"Since we're talking about Smitty and Charlie, I better volunteer some information about these two," added Jerry. "When me and my boys arrived at Dr. Fine's Office, Smitty and Charlie invited us out on the balcony to talk about a business deal. They wanted me and my boys to go into a business deal with them. I didn't want to have any part of that deal. They said that if we didn't work with them, they would go to the police and accuse me of killing the wrestler on the roof."

"What kind of deal did they want to make with you?" asked Columbo. "Just what kind of racket was they into?"

"They was trying to get the managers to sign their boys over to them," answered Jerry. "If they didn't, they wanted me and my boys to put the pressure on them to make them do it."

"Did you agree to work with them?" asked Stephen.

"I didn't want to go back to the slammer, so I'm afraid I did," answered Jerry. "It didn't go any further than that. You pretty much know what happened to me and the boys after that. You spent most of that time playing Junior Detective, accusing me of murder by playing twenty questions. You did keep me on my toes by having to come up with the right answers. For a boxer, I would say you did a pretty good job. If I was really guilty of these crimes, you would have had me."

"Awe, it twasn't nothing. I would have done that for anybody I thought was the killer.

Rex, I would like to stay for a while. I have a funny feeling that our problems aren't over," insisted Stephen. "If this Dr. Nejino is working with Dr. Fine, something is wrong. Somehow I think all these people are working together. I don't know, but I'm sure they're up to something. I think we should all keep out of sight and stay together here at Columbo's house, with his permission until we know for sure."

"You're safety comes first, so you're all welcome to stay," offered Columbo. "Rex, where do you think we should go from here?"

"Who do we have left in this mysterious situation? I think I can compare them to have the madness of brothers who think they are each a genius" observed Rex. "First we have Dr. Fine who is an author and a hypnotist. Next we have Michael The Magnificent, alias Dr. Nejino who works with spooks. And last we have Charlie The Chill who threatens managers of wrestlers to sign over their boys to him. Each of them live in there own world created by their own egos.

I think I should let Margret go get a treatment from Dr. Nejino to see how he ties in with everything. Jerry if you still want to help, I want to take you to the captain about making you a Detective."

"Sure, I still want to be a Detective and help," answered Jerry. "Other than my friends, you, Columbo and Stephen are the only ones to give me an even brake. I'll never forget this."

"Good," replied Rex. "That will make my plan perfect, because I want you and Stephen to get involved with Charlie and the wrestlers since you already have a deal with him. Maybe we can turn up some new information about the dead wrestler on the roof."

"What can I do to help," asked Ace.

"If Dixie is willing to help, I want you, Lefty, Danny, Shorty and Mugs to stay with her and protect her, replied Rex. "Dixie, I want you to continue helping Dr. Fine and see what else you can find out about Dr. Nejino. By the way, where is Scooter?"

"Oh he went down to his bedroom to work with his chemicals," answered Hannibal. "He said he was going to mix his chemicals together to make him some vitamins."

"He isn't going to drink those chemicals?" asked Rex as Scooter was sitting at a desk in his bedroom.

"Now let's see," observed Scooter. "This time I'm going to mix the blue with the green in my metal milk shake can. Then I'm going to add a little red and yellow. No, that's not right. I need more red just like the color of the brick. Now to put a little brown in it. That really looks good. Now it's time to shake it up and then have a drink. That's really tastes good," said Scooter and then he squeezed the metal can together with one hand. Then he picked up his red brick, squeezing it into pieces. "These vitamins really make you strong," laughed Scooter just as Hannibal entered the room.

"What happened to your brick?" asked a curious Hannibal.

"My vitamins. I was holding my brick in my hand and squeezed it too hard. My beautiful brick," cried Scooter. "Now I have to ask Janet for another brick."

"You did that with one hand?" asked a surprised Hannibal. "What do you mean, vitamins. Just what's going on here? What did you do?"

"I made me some vitamins and drank them. They really work. They are good for you and really make you strong," explained Scooter.

"What are you doing drinking chemicals?" asked Hannibal. "I ought to let you have it."

Grabbing Hannibal by the shirt and picking him up in the air, Scooter replied, "Temper, temper. Don't forger, I'm an Honorary Detective and you are my assistant. I'm your boss. If you try to hurt me, I'm going to report you to Uncle Columbo."

"OK, just let me down. I promise I won't hurt you," pleaded Hannibal. "You stay here. I have to go upstairs to get something to drink."

"Would you like me to mix up some of my vitamins for you to drink?" asked Scooter.

"No, I would rather have a cola," reasoned Hannibal as he rushed out of the bedroom.

As Hannibal went upstairs to join Columbo and his guests Hannibal announced to everyone, "Stephen, the last thing I heard you say after I went downstairs to check on Scooter, that you didn't think our problems aren't over. You may think that Dr. Nejino and Dr. Fine may be causing more problems. You may not think this is unusual for Scooter. I think he has a surprise for all of us. You'll never guess what he's done this time."

"Now what's he done?" asked Columbo.

"I sure want to know," exclaimed Rex. "Is this something we have to hide from Margret?"

"Did his ants get loose again?" laughed Ace.

"No it's a chemical problem," explained Hannibal. "Scooter mixed some chemicals together and he calls them vitamins."

"So what's wrong with that?" asked Stephen.

"I'll tell you what's wrong," replied Hannibal. "Scooter has the appetite of a horse and the jaws of a chicken. He drank those chemicals."

"Did that turn him into a forty inch small fry?" laughed Rex. "If it did, I want Margret to see that."

"It may be worst than that. Those chemicals he calls vitamins made him very strong," Hannibal continued to say. "Scooter doesn't even know how strong he is. For some people, it may be very difficult to pick up a pumpkin with one finger. I saw Scooter grab his brick and he crushed it with one hand. After that he grabbed my shirt and picked me up off the floor like I was a piece of paper. He thought I was going to hurt him. He told me if I did, he was going to tell Uncle Columbo."

"Is this unfounded strength going to be permanent?" asked Columbo. "I sure hope not."

"I think Ace will need to drink Scooter's vitamins so he can beat me when we box," laughed Stephen.

"I don't need his vitamins," laughed Ace. "If you remember correctly, I was going to hit you in the head with a brick, a very red brick."

"I hear Scooter coming up the steps. Let's keep talking about our friendly doctors and then see what Scooter does," instructed Columbo.

"Dixie, does Margret plan on seeing Dr. Nejino?" asked Rex.

"No, by the time you got to Dr. Fines, she wasn't able to make that decision," answered Dixie.

"I'm hungry," said Scooter as he entered the room as Rex was talking.

"I'll fix you something to eat," replied Janet. "You must be hungry after taking a nap?"

"I wasn't taking a nap," answered Scooter. "I was making some vitamins with my chemicals."

"Your kidding," replied Rex. "Just how do you go about making vitamins with your chemicals? Maybe we should put your vitamins in bottles and sell it."

"I'll tell you how I made my vitamins," replied Scooter. "It was very easy. First I mixed the blue with the green. Then I put red and yellow in my can. I added more red so I would have a brick red. The last thing I added was brown and then I shook the chemicals around in my can really good and I drank it."

"You what?" asked Rex.

"I drank it and now my vitamins make me feel really good," explained Scooter. "Janet, the bricks you have aren't made very good. I picked up my brick with one hand and it crumbled. It must have gotten damaged when I dropped it on Dr. Zodiac's foot. I don't know why he got mad because I dropped an inferior brick on his foot? It was my brick that got damaged."

"How would you like to help me out on another case, Honorary Detective Scooter?" asked Rex. "The way you took down Dr. Zodiac with your brick, we can sure use your help again."

"Of course I would. What are my orders, sir?" asked Scooter. "Will I need more bricks?"

"I don't think so. This is going to be different than chasing that little weasel, Dr. Zodiac with a brick. If your vitamins are what you say they are, you might need them," replied Rex. "We think Charlie The Chill is breaking the law. How would you like to work with Stephen and Jerry on this case?"

"Will Hannibal still be my assistant and do everything I say?" asked Scooter.

"Hannibal will be your assistant, but this time he will be taking orders from Stephen the same as you will," explained Rex.

"What kind of orders will Stephen be giving? Will he be ordering pizzas or sandwiches?" laughed Scooter.

"If your nice, really nice, I may order you a nice new red brick," laughed Stephen.

"Well it better be made a lot better than the last brick I had. Maybe you should get a different brand," Scooter went on to say.

"Exactly, You got it," answered Stephen. "I buy nothing but the best for my buddy."

"Stephen, now that Scooter is taking his vitamins, I think you know what kind of assignment you should give him," hinted Rex. "To begin with, call Charlie The Chill and remind him of your partnership about the managers and wrestlers you agreed upon.

When he last saw you and Stephen, he may believe that you two are far from friends. Tell him that you and Stephen were at odds with boxing, because he wouldn't take a fall. There is something you know from his past that can put him in jail. You told him to accept a partnership with us or you would give this information to the police. Stephen said he would accept this partnership if he could include his friends, Hannibal and Scooter."

"With his friend Smitty The Grim Reaper gone, I'm sure he will go for this because with this kind of racket, he won't want to work alone," replied Jerry.

"Then why don't you, Stephen, Hannibal and Scooter sit on one side of this room and discuss plans for a strategy while Columbo, Dixie and I figure out how to approach Dr. Fine and Dr. Nejino?" suggested Rex.

Before you get started, come out to the kitchen and get some more food," offered Janet. "There is an awful lot of left overs."

Chapter Eighteen
Operation Wrestler

The next morning, Jerry and Dixie appeared to move back to their apartments in the hotel as if everything was back to normal. It was now 9:00 a. m. and Jerry, Dixie and the gang was eating breakfast in Jerry's apartment and then there was a knock on the door.

"He's right on time," yelled Ace. "Come on in Charlie. We're all having breakfast. Would you care for something to eat?"

"Maybe I'll have a cup of coffee," replied Charlie. "I can wait until everyone is done eating before we get started."

"I have one item of business to take care of, before we start," explained Jerry. "With Smitty gone, I think we should replace him with a new partner, that is experienced in our type of business."

"There is something you should know before we add any new partners," explained Charlie. "I am already working with somebody else who wishes to remain a silent partner. I don't think we need any new partners."

"That changes everything," replied Jerry. "I don't want to get involved in a racket like this if I don't know everybody I'm working with. I've already been to the slammer once. I don't want to take any chances of a silent partner turning on me."

"I'll tell you what. You tell me who you have in mind and I will consider making him a partner if you let me keep my silent partner," reasoned Charlie. "Right now you have several people working with you. Now that Smitty is gone, there is just me."

"It's somebody we all know and hate. Would you believe it's our friend, World Middle Weight Boxing Champion, Stupid Stunning Stephen Edwards," answered Jerry.

"But he's a boxing champion and a Detective," replied Charlie. "He isn't by far my choice. He's not even a good fit. I don't want a partner that's going to put me in the slammer. Have you been eating local weed? I'm releasing you of our partnership. No way. I'm out of here."

"I think you will change your mind after I tell you the rest," explained Jerry. "You and I made a deal and I'm making you stick to it. To begin with, you didn't tell me you had a silent partner. Now your telling me that you have a silent partner. Just hear me out and I'm sure you'll change your mind about letting Stephen in on our deal.

I haven't said anything to Stephen yet and I know he is getting ready to leave town. I have found some incriminating evidence in Stephen's past that could very easily put him in the slammer and strip him of his World Middle Class Boxing Championship tittle. Since Stephen is familiar with this kind of sport, I'm sure he would rather be willingly be our partner instead of in the slammer."

"I think your on to something," offered Charlie. "Once he becomes our partner, his hands will start to get dirty and then we'll have him."

"If he becomes our partner, we'll have to include his two friends," added Jerry.

"If it's who I think it is, the deals off!" screamed Charlie. "Your talking about Hannibal and that nit wit Scooter. I would rather go to the slammer than to be around a person who walks around with bricks. There was an article in this mornings paper called, "The Brick vs Dr. Zodiac". Then it said something about Dr. Zodiac drinking some chemicals Scooter made up and he turned into a forty inch small fry. Nobody can turn into a forty inch small fry from drinking chemicals."

"I'm afraid you're wrong," insisted Jerry. "Me and my gang did after Ace had the boxing match with Scooter just before we went to prison. Stephen Edwards drank some chemicals that made him invisible. Everybody thought it was Scooter boxing with Ace, when it was really an invisible Stephen Edwards doing the boxing."

"I think you're all nuts. I just want out of this deal," pleaded Charlie.

"This is all for real," answered Ace. "I seen it with my own eyes. Scooter has now come up with a formula that he calls vitamins. After he drinks this formula, he becomes so strong, he can crush a brick with one hand.

Don't you see the possibilities as to how this can fit in our racket? That's another reason we need Stephen, Hannibal and Scooter in on this deal. We're in this all the way. You can join us or compete against us. Before we let you compete against us, we're going to run you out of Davenport just like we did before."

"I guess when you put it that way, I'm in," pleaded a nervous Charlie. "What do you plan to do next?"

"I guess since you're here, I'll call the boys and have them join us right away," replied Jerry. "Next we need to discuss our plans as a newly formed organization as to how we're to proceed while we are waiting for them to arrive."

Thirty minutes later, Stephen, Hannibal and Scooter had joined the gang at Jerry's apartment.

"Stephen, Hannibal and Scooter, now that you're here, I am going to explain to you about your part in this newly profitable organization," explained Jerry. "Each of you have the special talents we need to make this all work. Stephen, for the last couple of days you have been trying to hang the rap of murder on me. Now that you know I'm in the clear, it's time to get your hands dirty."

"I'm not exactly sure what this is all about," replied Stephen. "Now I have a new life, because I've worked hard to get this new boxing tittle and I don't want to loose it."

"Sure you know what this is about and you won't loose you're tittle if you do what I tell you," answered Jerry. "This time I'm into wrestling instead of boxing. I always said you look like a guy who knows what time it is, because you know your way around. I want you to help us to get the managers of the wrestlers to sign their boys over to us.

127

Next I want you and Hannibal to act as Scooter's wrestling managers. I happened to know that Scooter drinks vitamins from his chemical mixture and it makes him very strong. We need to get him in the ring to wrestle, because he is a natural."

"Wait," replied Scooter. "Nobody told me that I was going to have to wrestle. Is Stephen going to be invisible and help me? Otherwise I could get hurt."

"Hannibal and I aren't going to let you get hurt," insisted Stephen. "Did I let you get hurt when you boxed Ace?"

"Ace did hit me in the face and knocked me out. I don't want to do this," screamed Scooter.

"How about if I helped Stephen and Hannibal train you," offered Ace. "Just like Stephen and Hannibal, I'm not going to let you get hurt. When you and I had our boxing match, I know I hit you and I'm very sorry. I always believe that doing a good turn for somebody else makes you feel good all year and I would be lost without it. Would you let me help train you, so I can make it up to you?"

"Scooter, you know I have always tried to protect you all your life," explained Hannibal. "You just don't have any idea how strong you get after you drink your vitamins. It's your opponent that's going to get hurt, because of your strength and he just can't hurt you. You really have a short memory, don't you. All of us was extremely scared of Dr. Zodiac. You stood up to him with your nice red brick and chased him around the hotel. Now you've got your vitamins that makes you very strong and you can chase your wrestling opponent around the ring."

"Yes I was chasing that Dr. Zodiac around the hotel," boomed Scooter. "If I decide to do this, who would I wrestle?"

"Well, there are three wrestlers at the beginning of the list," responded Charlie. "There is Barney, The Bone Crusher, Jake, The Jack Hammer and Barry, The Buzz Saw. I need you to get in the ring and beat these wrestlers so we can get the managers to sign these wrestlers over to us."

"Their name makes them sound very mean to me," reasoned Scooter. "I don't think I want to do this."

"Oh that's just their nick name, just like your nick name is Scooter and Hannibal is his nick name. These wrestlers use these nick names to sound kind of tough because it's their specialty. They have to sound mean to get people to buy tickets to see them wrestle," explained Stephen. "Everything about Dr. Zodiac sounded scary, but you stood up to him."

"Well, I don't like scary names," answered Scooter. "If I wrestle, I want to be called Scooter, The Stupid."

"If you want to win these matches, a scary name will help. That sounds fine if Scooter, The Stupid is something you would want to be called," laughed Stephen. "I guess that makes you one of a kind."

"With a name like that, your opponent won't know what to expect from you," laughed Ace. "Between your ants and your bricks, who knows what you'll think of next."

"That's my buddy," added Hannibal. "You never know what to expect from Scooter. Scooter is a very good person and he will always be my best friend."

"I agree," added Stephen. "That is why we should all take special care that he doesn't ever get hurt."

"I think I'm going to take these wrestlers aside before the match and explain to them the benefits of not hurting Scooter," exclaimed Ace.

"I just don't know what to say," cried Scooter. "I thought because I always did something stupid, it would make people hate me. That settles it. The wrestling name I choose because if my passions with bricks will be Scooter, The Brick."

"Scooter is going to wrestle these men," laughed Charlie. "I just don't know who to feel sorry for, the wrestlers that Scooter is going to face or Scooter. I said earlier that I would rather go to the slammer instead of being in on this deal with Scooter. This puts a new light on our deal.

These three wrestlers along with their managers that I mentioned have really been giving me a hard time. Now that we have Scooter with his vitamins, as our own wrestler, they are going to be in for a big surprise. I just hope that Scooter's vitamins really work."

"You catch on fast. Believe me, they really work," added Hannibal. "Think of Scooter as a wild bird that we want to sing. If we want Scooter to sing, we can't put him in a cage. In Scooter's case, after he drinks his vitamins, we will put him in a ring to wrestle. These wrestlers won't know about his vitamins and how strong they make him. Scooter at first didn't know how strong it made him. I really saw him crush a brick with one hand."

"I just thought my vitamins tasted good and made me feel good," explained Scooter. "I thought Dr. Zodiac wrecked my brick when it fell on his foot. I had no idea that my vitamins made me so strong at I could crush a brick with one hand."

"Your learning. Now I think your starting to understand how strong you are after you drink your vitamins," replied Hannibal. "Your not going to be the one getting hurt. It's more like Barney, The Bone Crusher, Jake, The Jack Hammer and Barry, The Buzz Saw that is going to end up in a lot of pain."

"When I wrestle these men, do I really have to hurt them," cried Scooter. "I'm not mad at them. I don't even know them."

"No, you won't have to hurt them my friend. I promise you, you won't regret this decision. You can never go wrong by giving the other person an even brake. You have a good heart, because you are always thinking of others. You always keep your word, value the truth by playing fair and square and help folks when they need you," answered Stephen.

"You mean when I'm doing things like that, it isn't stupid?" asked Scooter.

"No Scooter, these ideas are far from being stupid," answered Stephen. "You can never go wrong with ideas like that. Just think of wrestling as a game that you are trying to win. Ace, Hannibal and myself will teach you how to wrestle without hurting anyone. Just remember keeping an open mind will keep you moving forward."

Everyday for the next two weeks, Scooter was taught how to wrestle by his friends at Jerry's Gym on Elmore Avenue in Davenport. Keeping Jerry informed of Scooter's progress, as he trained at Jerry's gym, Jerry called Charlie to set up a match between Scooter, The Brick and Barney, The Bone Crusher.

"I really want Barney's Manager, to sign his boy up with me," insisted Charlie.

"Correction, you mean to say that you want Barney's Manager to sign up with us," scolded Jerry. "Don't forget, we made a deal as partners and we're all in it to make a buck or two."

"I know," replied Charlie. "I didn't mean to say it that way. I'm just used to having Smitty as my partner and now he's gone, because of Dr. Zodiac. Let me hang up so I can call Barney's manager."

"When you set that match up, inform Barney's manager that match will take place at my gym," added Jerry. "With the ticket sales, by using my gym, we'll make more money than if we was to hold the match somewhere else. We also need to sign up other wrestlers to fill in the card for that night. While you're at it, set up matches with Jake, The Jack Hammer and Barry, The Buzz Saw."

"Will I have to wrestle all these men at the same time?" asked a puzzled Scooter.

"Eventually, but not on the same night. You're only allowed to send one wrestler to the hospital at a time," laughed Jerry.

"I'm not going to wrestle if I have to hurt anyone," scolded Scooter.

"I was just joking with you. Your not going to hurt anyone," promised Jerry. "In fact, I have a great idea. After you get into the ring you can do some funny stuff, that's funny and clean. Before you start to wrestle, you can begin to sing and scare these wrestlers off by breaking into a dance called The Brick."

"I never heard of a dance called The Brick," replied Scooter.

"I'm sure that Dixie can help you make one up. To start with, you can jump up and down on one foot and then the other," suggested Jerry. "Here is an example of what you can also do. As you're jumping up and down, you can sing, "Ouch, ouch. I'm Dr. Zodiac. I'm in pain, you lame brain, you idiot. Whoever walks around with a brick must be insane. If you can make these wrestlers laugh, that would make them momentarily vulnerable."

"You mean like Dr. Zodiac did after I dropped my brick on his foot?" questioned Scooter. "Only Dr. Zodiac didn't laugh. He was very mad, because I hurt his foot."

"That's exactly what I mean. He was still momentarily vulnerable and because of that, you got the best of him. Now how does that sound to you?" asked Jerry.

"Now it sounds like it's going to be fun to wrestle. I'll do it," vowed Scooter. "It's a lot better to have fun instead of hurting people.

When I was a kid in school, I did a lot of stupid things and the other kids made fun of me and they would beat me up. People always made fun of Joan of Arc, but she went ahead and built it anyway.

I was hurt so deeply that I made up my mind to never hurt anybody else, no matter what. I believed as long as I could laugh, it would keep me safe from the world. I also learned that laughter kept me safe from myself, because I was always doing stupid things. I never made insulted people with jokes about anybody's big ears, their stut-terin or about them being a nut."

"What's going on here?" asked Charlie. "Just what is all this nonsense about singing and dancing at a wrestling match. This isn't suppose to be a musical special. This is about two men wrestling, fighting it out to win the match and Barney, The Bone Crusher is a tough wrestler. He has never lost a match. Scooter better win so we can put pressure on Barney's manager to sign Barney over to us. My silent partner will insist on this."

"I know," replied Jerry. "My partners and I want to make some serious money at this. We're not new at this. We know exactly what we're doing."

After Charlie left, Stephen remarked to everybody, "It looks like we have a wrestler to train. Hannibal, why don't you report to Rex and Columbo about our progress into the dealings of Charlie, with the wrestlers and their managers and then meet us at Jerry's Gym.

I think this will really help this case, now that we know Charlie has a silent partner. Our problem is to find out who this silent partner is, because it can be anybody.

Scooter, you are part of our team and because you are representing us as our wrestler, your going to be the key in helping us solve this case."

"Do you really think so? Although I'm scared to death to wrestle, I want to help solve this case," answered Scooter.

"True courage is when you're scared to death and you still face your opponent," explained Stephen. "You need to do what must be done by being tough and courageous. If you want to win a fight, you need to get up one more time than you've been knocked down."

"This is very difficult for me and because I don't want to do this, I don't want to get hurt or hurt anybody else" replied Scooter. "I don't want you to be disappointed in me. I may be hopelessly lazy and good for nothing. I'll do the best I can."

"I know you will. You're my buddy and a good person. I know I can always depend on you," answered Stephen.

Chapter Nineteen
Scooter The Brick

It is now a week later. Stephen, Ace, Jerry and Hannibal are in Scooter's dressing room at Jerry's Gym.

"How are you feeling, Scooter?" Are you ready to wrestle Barry, The Bone Crusher?" asked Stephen.

"I think I'm ready," said a nervous Scooter. "Hannibal, would you hand me my jar of vitamins? After I drink my vitamins I should be ready."

"Did you practice the dance that Dixie made up for you?" asked Jerry.

"Ya, I practiced it," replied Scooter. "It seems like a stupid dance, so it should be fine."

"I have a present for you," offered Ace. "It's a nice red plastic brick you can carry into the ring with you. Before you start your dancing and singing, when the referee tells both of you to shake hands, you can let the brick slip out of your hands and let it fall on Barry's foot. That should soften him up a little before you start to wrestle."

"I wish I had brought my chemicals for Barry to drink that would turn Barry into a forty inch small fry," insisted Scooter.

"No, no, no," jested Stephen. "This is just a game of two tough men battling it out in the ring. You don't need any chemicals since you have your brick. Then remember, you have your singing and dancing going for you. Now grab your brick. It's time to go meet your first opponent."

A couple minutes later, Scooter was climbing in the ring with his manager and trainers right behind him. As he stood there in his corner of the ring, he looked over at Barry, who had a ferocious look on his face.

"I want to go home. I forgot something," said a frightened Scooter.

"Just what did you forget?" asked Stephen. "Everything you need is right here."

"I forgot to stay there," answered Scooter as he attempted to make his way out of the ring.

"I'm really ashamed of you for wanting to leave. Now you stay in this ring and box. I mean wrestle," replied an angry Hannibal. "We spent all this time working with you. You said you was going to help us solve this case and now your going to stay and wrestle."

"I hate wrestling, especially when I have to do it. Look how big that guy is over there with a mean look on his face. How can I be nice to that angry man?" replied Scooter.

"That's enough, Scooter. Just do what we told you. He's just trying to scare you so that he can win this game of wrestling. We didn't spend all this time training you so you get hurt and lose. After you drop the brick on his foot, he will be like a pussy cat. You will have him running for his life," instructed Stephen. "After the announce introduces both of you, go to the center of the ring. The referee will be waiting for you and take your brick with you."

A minute later Scooter was standing in the center of the ring with his brick, facing Barry, The Bone Crusher as the referee explained to the wrestlers the standard rules of wrestling.

After the referee was done, he said, "OK, shake hands and then go to your corners and come out with a good clean fight."

"Scooter immediately put out his right hand to shake as planned as the plastic brick fell on Barry's foot and then said, "You can't go wrong if you start each day with a song."

Then Scooter went into his dance, jumping up and down on one foot, then the other and began to sing as the audience began to laugh, "Ouch, ouch. I'm Dr. Zodiac. I'm in pain, you lame brain. You idiot. Who ever walks around with a brick must be insane."

Hearing Scooter sing and seeing him jump up and down dancing on one foot then the other, Barry turned around in a big hurry to go back to his corner.

"Start the wrestling! Start the wrestling!" yelled Scooter. "You're suppose to wrestle me, not chase it all over the ring."

Barry then continued to walk faster, tripping and as he fell he hit his head on the metal ring post.

The referee walked over to Barney and counted to ten and then pronounced Barry out.

"Will a doctor come up to the ring?" yelled the referee. "Barry, The Bone Crusher is really hurt."

After the doctor proceeded to examine Barry, he told Barry's manager to call an ambulance.

The announcer then called Scooter to the center of the ring. The referee grabbed Scooter by the right arm and raised it as the announcer said, "Without laying a hand on Barry, The Bone Crusher, Scooter, The Brick wins the match."

"You did it!" yelled Stephen. "You won and you didn't even hurt the guy. He tripped and did it to himself!"

Chapter Twenty
WE'VE GOT PROBLEMS

It was 8:00 a. m. the next morning and the phone rang at Jerry's apartment. It was Charlie calling in desperation.

"Jerry, we've got problems, big problems," boomed Charlie. "I need to meet with you and your partners as soon as possible. Can we meet at 9:00 a. m. at your apartment?"

"What kind of problems?" replied Jerry.

"I'll tell you when I get there. Just have your people there at 9:00 a. m.," answered Charlie.

It is now 9:00 a. m. and there is a knock on the door at Jerry's apartment. It was Charlie standing there in a big sweat.

"You look terrible Charlie. Come on in and I'll get you something to drink," offered Jerry.

A minute later, Charlie was sitting on the sofa with a drink in his hand.

"Is that drink helping you relax as you are sitting on the couch?" asked Jerry.

"A little," replied Charlie. "I have a bottle of strong pain pills marked Scooter in my medicine cabinet that I've been taking since Scooter started his training as a wrestler."

"Now what's the big emergency?" insisted Jerry. "Scooter won the match last night. We should be celebrating."

"The problem isn't about Scooter winning the match. It's how he did it," explained Charlie. "I told you I had a silent partner. What I didn't tell you was that I don't know who he is. He was at the wrestling match last night and he was very unhappy what he saw."

"Now how can winning make anybody unhappy?" asked a confused Jerry.

"My silent partner called me at home after the match. After he hung up, I rushed to the medicine cabinet to take these pills, marked Scooter," responded Charlie. "My silent partner said he didn't like Scooter's singing and dancing, because he was making fun of Dr. Zodiac."

"Why should he care? Dr. Zodiac is dead. I saw him at the bottom of the elevator shaft, dead as a door nail," reasoned Stephen.

"According to my silent partner, Dr. Zordiac is not dead. He still has a score to settle with all of you," insisted Charlie. "He says he wrote a letter to all of you about how he plans you're demise. If Scooter does this same musical number in any more matches, he will be wrestling with death. He will add Scooter to the list of people in his letter and his life will also be in peril."

"You don't say. You don't say," exclaimed Scooter. "Tell him if he's going to scare me with his threats, it worked."

"Dr. Zodiac is dead. He killed people the same way a coward would do," protested Ace. "He hid in the corner of a dark room at Dr. Fine's demonstration and killed two innocent men with poison darts and then fled the murder scene like a scarred y cat. He woke up two defenseless women in their sleep, scaring them out of their wits by threatening them. Then he wrote us all a threatening letter and shoved it under the door of this apartment. I repeat, he's a coward and I challenge him to face me if he is really still alive. That goes the same for your silent partner."

"My silent partner also threatened me if I don't get Scooter to stop his singing and dancing," replied Charlie. "As a partner, I demand that Scooter stop this. If Scooter does this again, I will be in great danger, since I don't know who my silent partner is."

"I'll tell you what," suggested Stephen. "Why don't you leave town for a while and don't tell anybody where you're going? Check back with me after Scooter wrestles the next two men. If your silent partner has any issues with Scooter, tell him to contact me, because Scooter is going to continue his song and dance routine."

"OK, I'll leave town. It doesn't look good for me, so I don't have a choice," roared Charlie.

"Charlie, can I go with you?" asked Scooter. "It's been a while since I've had a vacation."

"You're not going anywhere," insisted Hannibal. "You have two men that you have to wrestle."

"How about if I give you my vitamins to drink and then you can have your chance to wrestle them?" pleaded Scooter. "You can even have my plastic brick to drop on their feet."

"You're going to have to stay here. Charlie doesn't want your company," replied Hannibal. "If he took you with him, he would be doing something stupid. Just how would that make you feel?"

"Smarter than Charlie," answered Scooter. "I'm sorry Charlie. I can't go with you. You have to go without me."

Later that day, Stephen and the gang went back to Columbo's house and reported to Rex and Columbo about their meeting with Charlie.

"What have you got to report?" asked Rex.

"It looks like we have really upset Charlie's silent partner by hitting on some of his nerves with Scooter's wrestling," exclaimed Stephen. "His silent partner was at Scooter's match last night. It turns out that he doesn't like Scooter's singing and dancing. He says that Scooter is making fun of Dr. Zodiac and he claims that Dr. Zodiac is not dead.

He says that Dr. Zodiac still has a score to settle with all of us. If Scooter doesn't quit his musical act, he's going to add Scooter to the list of people mentioned in the letter. What Charlie failed to tell us about his silent partner is that Charlie has no idea who his silent partner is."

"This is a complete surprise to me," noted Rex. "I knew there was something funny going on here. We all saw the body of Dr. Zodiac or at least who we thought was Dr. Zodiac dead at the bottom of the elevator shaft. There must be some truth to what he's telling Charlie, because how would he know about the threatening letter Dr. Zodiac shoved under Jerry's apartment door?"

"To be on the safe side it looks like Janet and I are going to be having company for a bit longer," offered Columbo. "Stephen, it's a good thing you brought your funny feelings to our attention about something not being right. If we had gone back to our normal lives, and there is something to do with Dr. Zodiac still being alive, he may have just delivered his promise and caught up with some of us."

"I don't know why I had those feelings. I guess it's because I have trained myself to try and feel out the opposition when I box," replied Stephen.

"It's lucky for us that you can," reasoned Columbo. "I guess that makes you a better Detective than Rex and me."

"No, I just it was just a lucky guess. That's all there is to it," replied an embarrassed Stephen.

"There's no luck to it. You understand that the challenges that come your way is just reality. I think your just as good as a Detective as you are as a boxer, because you know that reality isn't fixed by wishing it away," answered Columbo. "Rex and I really appreciate you taking your time away from boxing to help us solve this case."

"Uncle Columbo, what do we do next?" asked Hannibal.

"Now that we know that Charlie's silent partner will be at Scooter's matches, we need to adjust, adapt and revise. To succeed in solving this case, we have to remain flexible and seize what opportunities that come along. I think it's time for Rex and myself with some other Detectives to be there at the next wrestling match as well," explained Uncle Columbo. "Maybe, we might just get lucky and catch this silent partner of Charlie's. I am very anxious to find out what he knows about Dr. Zodiac."

"Now that we're this far along, I think it's time to take Margret in to Dr. Fine's for another treatment," explained Rex.

"Does Margret know that we're investigating Dr. Fine and Dr. Nejino about possibly being connected to Dr. Zordiac and these murders?" asked Stephen.

"Not so loud. Margret's in the other room," whispered Rex. "Let's go outside where Margret can't hear us."

A couple minutes later the gang was outside away from the house as they talked about their plans with Margret and the doctors.

"I want to get an appointment for Margret to see Dr. Fine before the next wrestling match," Rex went on to say. "Margret doesn't need to know anything we suspect about Dr. Fine or Dr. Nejino, because then she wouldn't go to see Dr. Fine. If she did go, she might be so nervous that she would give things away. I'm going to have Dixie make an appointment for Margret to see Dr. Fine tomorrow morning."

"Since this is an investigation about Dr. Fine's and Dr. Nejino's possible involvement in a crime, are you going to be responsible for the $500.00 dollar treatment for Dr. Fine?" asked Stephen.

"No, the department will take cover of these expenses," replied Rex. "I am going to ask Dr. Fine if the insurance company will cover these treatments to see where that goes."

Chapter Twenty One
MARGRET'S TREATMENTS

The next morning, Rex, Margret, Columbo and Dixie entered Dr. Fine's Office.

"Hello everybody," greeted Dr. Fine. Looking at Margret, Dr. Fine asked, "How is my favorite patient doing today?"

"I'm sleeping good and have been very happy since my last treatment," replied Margret. "The truth is, I don't know what you are treating me for."

"You was really in bad shape the first time you came to me. That's what these treatments are for. You're not suppose to know, because I hypnotized you," reasoned Dr. Fine. "I'm going to hypnotize you again to reinforce the last treatment I gave you. When I'm done reinforcing the treatment, I am going to refer you to Dr. Nejino to take over."

"Will the insurance company pay for your treatments?" asked Rex. "I'm just a plain old Detective. $500.00 is a lot of money to pay for each treatment."

"No, I'm afraid not. I just hypnotize people. Although I go by the name of Dr. Fine, I am not considered a real doctor by any insurance company," answered Dr. Fine. "I know it's expensive, but my time is valuable. Hypnotizing people is my bread and butter. If I can help this dear lady for $500.00 with every treatment, it should be worth the money for you and your wife."

"I understand," replied Rex. "Even though it's expensive, here's $500.00. Now you can go ahead with the next treatment."

Looking at the $500.00, with excitement in his eyes, Dr. Fine then said, "Margret, come over here and sit in this chair by my desk, as you did before. Dixie, I need your assistance again. Give me one of your shinny ear rings and then help Margret get comfortable.

Margret, now that your relaxed, I want you to watch this ear ring, go back and forth back and forth. Your eye lids are getting droopy. Your beginning to sleep, sleep, sleep. You can only hear the sound of my voice as you sleep deeper, deeper, deeper. There is a man known as Scooter. You don't know who he is, because he's a stranger to you. When he talks to you, you don't hear him. When he's around you, you don't see him. Your a happy woman and you feel good all of the time and you sleep good all of the time. When you wake up, you will have a great desire to make an appointment with Dr. Nejino. When I snap my fingers, you will wake up. Margret, how do you feel?"

"I feel great," answered Margret. "I don't know why, but your treatments make me feel so happy."

"I'm so glad to hear that," replied Dr. Fine. "Do you think I should be giving you anymore treatments?"

"Since your treatments worked, I don't think I need anymore," reasoned Margret. "For some strange reason, I need to make an appointment to see a Dr. Nejino. I don't know who he is or why I need to see him."

"He is my partner and has an office in a large house east of the corner of 6th and Gaines on top of the hill," answered Dr. Fine.

"I don't understand why I need to see Dr. Nejino. I feel good, because your treatments worked," objected a puzzled Margret.

"Just why does Margret need to see Dr. Nejino?" asked Rex. "How much are his treatments?"

"Dr. Nejino also charges $500.00 a treatment. He uses spooks to complete my treatments to make them stick," explained Dr. Fine.

"I don't think Margret needs anymore treatments. Because of your treatments, Margret is feeling fine. Get it. Feeling fine," laughed Rex. "I guess you don't get it. Now I'm starting to sound like Scooter. This is a joke Scooter cracked the day of your demonstration."

"Who's this Scooter you're talking about?" asked Margret.

"At this time you don't know any Scooter," answered Rex. "Dr. Fine, I already gave you $1,000.00 for two treatments and it's getting to be too expensive an a Detective's pay. Where would a $800.00 week Detective get enough money to pay for more treatments for Margret? The only way I could do that is to have a hot streak at the casino."

"As you can see, the treatments are working for Margret. You do need some help with your crazy jokes," replied Dr. Fine.

"Rex, I still want to make an appointment to see Dr. Nejino. Please make that appointment for me," pleaded Margret. "For some reason, I really need to see him. I'm feeling very good right now. I like being happy. I haven't felt this good for a long time."

"Alright Margret, if that's what you really want to do," promised Rex.

"Do you want me to call Dr. Nejino for you to make that appointment?" asked Dr. Fine. "I think he's at home right now."

"Didn't you tell me that his house is east of 6th and Gaines on top of the hill?" replied Rex.

"That's right. His house is east of 6th and Gaines on top of the hill," answered Dr. Fine.

"In that case, I think I'll take Margret to his house to meet him," insisted Rex. "We need to find out more about this Dr. Nejino to see if he can help Margret before we make an appointment. I understand that Dr. Nejino is also known as Michael, The Magnificent, who is a partner of yours. Why the two names?"

"That's right, he is my partner. He uses the name Dr. Nejino to make him seem more mysterious, because of the kind of work he does," explained Dr. Fine. "He also uses the name Michael, The Magnificent, because he likes fancy names. The name he was born with is Michael Bart Bobnick. He used to be some kind of doctor and had two women working for him, Mrs. McKay and Cher.

Most of patients thought the way he treated them was kind of spooky, because he was always looking down on them. They thought he was always trying going to try and pull the rug out from underneath them or some kind of fast one. Because he was always masked. It would seem that he was always afraid of getting a virus of some sort.

He never could look his patients in the eye, because he would always tell his patients to turn their head to the left and just when they started to get comfortable, he would tell his patients to turn their head to the right.

One thing led to another and he became Dr. Nejino and started treating his patients with spooks."

Twenty minutes later, Rex and Margret was sitting in front of Dr. Nejino's desk talking to him.

"It's good to see both of you," Dr. Nejino began to say. "Rex, I see you must have thought about my conversation with you at Dr. Fine's Hypnotic Demonstration about Margret's condition. What have you two decided to do?"

"Since Dr. Fine treated Margret twice by hypnotizing her, he thought to complete the treatments, she needed to make an appointment with you," explained Rex. "Each treatment is costing me $500.00. That's a lot of money on a Detective's pay. When I talked to you last time, you never told me that Margret had to start her treatments with Dr. Fine. Just what is it, you can do for Margret for $500.00 that Dr. Fine hasn't already done?"

"Margret really had a bad mental problem. What Dr. Fine told me is that Margret has had that condition for quite a while," replied Dr. Nejino. "The condition she was in takes time to heal. I have an opening tomorrow at 10:00 a. m. Can you come at that time?"

"Can my friends, Columbo and Dixie be present with Margret and me at that treatment just like they were when Dr. Fine hypnotized Margret?" asked Rex. "Margret can use the extra support."

"We're all here to help Margret. If they wish to come, that's fine with me. I can use Dixie to help me with the treatment," answered Dr. Nejino. "Would you care if Dr. Fine was also present? He hasn't any idea what I do, because he has never been to one of my treatments."

"As you say. We're all here to help Margret. He can come as long as Margret doesn't care and he doesn't charge another $500.00. What do you say, Margret?" asked Rex.

"He has helped me so far. I would like him to come if he wants to," offered Margret.

"Then it's settled. I'll see all of you here tomorrow at ten," replied Dr. Nejino.

It is finally 10:00 a. m. the next morning. Rex, Margret, Columbo and Dixie are sitting in Dr. Nejino's office at his home waiting for Dr. Fine. As Dr. Fine entered the office, Dr. Nejino instructed everybody to go into the next room where the treatment will be given.

"To begin with, I am going to lay on this small bed in front of my desk," Dr. Nejino began to say as everybody was seated to watch the treatment. "Dixie will tie my hands and legs together. She will blindfold me and then she will turn the lights out except for the small light behind my desk."

After Dixie finished tying up Dr. Nejino and the lights were turned off, a sheet and a baseball bat was seen flying through the air behind Margret, Rex, Columbo and Dr. Fine. Next a hand with just the bones showing hovered over Dr. Fine from behind and landed on his shoulder, scaring him. Not knowing what to do, Dr. fine put his arms around Columbo, who was sitting next to him and yelled for help.

"Get your hands off of me!" boomed Columbo. "What's the matter with you?"

"Ooh, ooh, ooh, there's a hand on my shoulder," gasped Dr. Fine as the hand floated away and landed on Columbo's shoulder.

Looking down at Dr. Fine's shoulder, Columbo shouted, "There's no hand on your shoulder!"

"That's because the hand is now on your shoulder," replied a very nervous Dr. Fine pointing to Columbo's shoulder.

Columbo then looked at the hand on his shoulder and then he gasped yelling to Rex for help as the hand floated out of sight.

"Will you two be quiet so Dr. Nejino can start Margret's treatment?" instructed Rex.

"But there's a hand on my shoulder," Columbo went on to say as he pointed to his shoulder.

Observing Columbo's shoulder, Rex answered, "There's no hand on your shoulder. Columbo, your a Police Detective and Dr. Fine, you are suppose to be in the business of treating people with their mental problems. You are two grown men, now sit there and be quite."

Dixie then began to say, "I want complete silence from everybody as we begin. There is great danger in what we are all about to see and hear. I must warn all of you that death is present. Dr. Nejino's body can play no part as to what happens here. The spirits will take over his body completely."

"A spirit is crying out, Dr. Nejino began to say. "There is a barrier in the way. I will try and remove the barrier. Just who are you? Are you there? Are you from another world? You can't be far away. We need to talk to you. What are you waiting for? The unbelievers must know that the spirit is trying to get through. It's the spirit of Dr. Zodiac. I command you to speak. My lips will speak your thoughts as they come to me. Speak you unhappy spirit."

"I am Dr. Zodiac. I believe in the super natural. I have a score to settle with all these people here in Dr. Nejino's Office. They all think that I am dead because I fell down the elevator shaft, but I am very much alive."

"How can you be alive?" Columbo broke in to ask. "Rex and I saw your body at the bottom of the elevator shaft, dead as a door nail."

"You might say that I got better," answered Dr. Zodiac. "You can cut off the tail of a dog, but it's still a dog. I am here to warn all of you that you can't escape me, because I am planning the demise of all of you. Even a smart man can mistake a bumble bee for a blackberry. Death is like an elephant that kneels under every gate. When the lights are turned back on, you will discover that I mean business."

"Dixie, turn the lights on and now!" demanded Rex.

As the lights were turned on, everybody saw Dr. Fine laying on the floor. Rushing over to Dr. Fine, Rex reached down to check Dr. Fine's pulse.

"He's dead," Rex said to everyone. "Now at taking a closer look, I can see a poisonous dart sticking in the back of his neck."

"Did I hear you right? How can Dr. Fine be dead?" asked Columbo. "That's a mystery to me because he was very much alive just seconds ago. Why would Dr. Zodiac want to kill Dr. Fine? He wasn't mentioned in the letter we got."

"The question is how was he killed and was it Dr. Zodiac who really killed him? Nobody else in this room could have killed him," exclaimed Rex. "Everybody has an air tight alibi because the dart is in back of Dr. Fine's neck. Everybody in this room was sitting either in front of or next to Dr. Fine. The killer is not going to escape this time.

I promise you one thing, if I don't get the rat who killed Dr. Fine, I'll turn in my badge. It takes a very clever man to bite into a pie without breaking its crust. Sooner or later we're going to find out just who the rat is that killed Dr. Fine and how."

"I'm getting to hate this place! Every time I come for a treatment, somebody dies!" cried Margret. "I'm not feeling good. I've had more than enough! Rex, take me home!"

Responding to Margret's urgent request, Rex asked Columbo, "Would you finish up here for me again? Lock the door to this room. Call an ambulance and the lab. You understand that I must take Margret home again? I never expected this to happen at Margret's treatment."

Fifteen minutes later, an ambulance pulled into the drive way of Dr. Nejino's home and the paramedics went inside.

"Where is the body?" asked one of the paramedics.

"It's in this other room," answered Columbo. "Wait and I'll unlock the door for you."

Entering the room, Columbo continued to say, "The body is right there on the floor with a poisonous dart sticking out of it's neck."

"Where's the body? I don't see a body," inquired the paramedic. "Will somebody tell me what's going one here? Are you trying to play another joke on us? You Detectives are crazy. The last time you called us to pick up a body, there wasn't a body. It's like the dead body got up and walked away. We've got more important things to do than going around to have jokes played on us."

"Dixie, Dr. Nejino, tell these men that there was a body, dead as a door nail laying here on the floor," instructed Columbo. "The door was locked and there was no way it could get out. That doesn't sound right. A body can't get up and walk away. What I mean to say was this door was securely locked and nothing could get in or out."

"There really was a body laying on the floor. I saw it and I don't understand what happened to the body. Things are getting spooky around here," exclaimed Dixie.

"Dr. Nejino, what can you tell us about the missing body?" asked the paramedic.

"As Dixie says, things are getting spooky around here. Of course it is, because I deal in spooks," replied Dr. Nejino. "If there was a body there like Dixie and Columbo say there was, the spooks was responsible for it's death and took it," explained Dr. Nejino. "I was blindfolded and tied up while I was giving a treatment to Margret Tarillo. Death is always present when I give these treatments."

"Either your all crazy or your all in on this Halloween joke together It remains to be seen," answered the paramedic. "In any case, we have to go."

The next morning the headlines in the local paper read,
"Dr. Preston Fine, Murdered Under Cops Noses"
"Detective T. J. Columbo and Detective Rex Tarillo attended a treatment with spooks, for Margret Tarillo, at Dr. Nejino's home where he has an office. The Detectives claim somebody murdered Dr. Preston Fine under their very noses. These are getting to be know as The Blow Gun Murders. A slow acting poisonous dart was found sticking out of the back of Dr. Fine's neck.

When the paramedics arrived to pick up the body of Dr. Preston Fine, there was no body to be found. This is the second time that paramedics were called to pick up a dead body that wasn't there.

This is also the second time in a couple of weeks that two other murders was committed. Two reporters from the media was also murdered with a poisonous dart sticking out of the back of their necks under the noses of these same cops. You would think that it would be harder to keep these murders a secret than it would be to bounce an egg off of a cement floor.

The cops are tight lipped about who they believe the suspect is at this time. It is rumored that they are confused, because they are wrestling with death. It's impossible to prove a murder was committed with out a body.

Their only explanation is that they believe the suspect is Dr. Zodiac who believes in the super natural. They think that Dr. Zodiac was responsible for the killings at Dr. Fine's Hypnotic Demonstration.

It is a known fact that Dr. Zodiac was found dead in the bottom of an elevator shaft at a local hotel. If Dr. Zodiac somehow still is alive, it remains to be seen.

Dead bodies disappearing. Dead bodies coming alive. Treatments with spooks. This all sounds creepy and scary. Could this be a publicity stunt to promote Halloween now that it's getting closer? That remains to be seen."

Chapter Twenty Two
THE SEARCH FOR THE SILENT PARTNER

It was finally Saturday night, about a week later. Scooter and the gang was again in Scooter's dressing room getting Scooter ready to fight Jake, The Jack Hammer. As Stephen was instructing Scooter how to fight Jake, The Jack Hammer, they heard the announcer calling for Scooter to come out to the ring. A couple minutes later Scooter was again in his corner of the ring. Rex, Columbo and two other Detectives was sitting in the audience, hoping to discover who Charlie's silent partner is.

"Here is your brick. Now go out in the center of the ring where the referee and Jake, The Jack Hammer is," instructed Stephen.

"He looks meaner than Barry, The Bone Crusher," insisted Scooter. "Are you sure I can't leave so I can go find Charlie?"

"Get out there," scolded Hannibal. "Maybe you would like to wrestle me?"

"OK, I'm going. I'm going. You don't have to be nasty about it," cried Scooter.

Again Scooter was in the center of the ring facing the referee and this time Jake, The Jack Hammer.

After the referee was done giving instructions to the wrestlers, Jake The Jack Hammer pulled out a real brick he was hiding in his left hand from behind his back and held it up to Scooter.

"If you want to use bricks to wrestle with, I decided to teach you a lesson about using a brick in a wrestling match, so I bring my own," Jake remarked. "I can sing and dance just like you. I'm not going to drop the brick on your foot. I'm going to smash it on your head."

"Scooter immediately grabbed the brick out of Jake's hand and took a closer look at it.

"That sure is a nice red brick," exclaimed Scooter as he squeezed the brick. "That looks better than the one I dropped on Dr. Zodiac's foot. Correction, that brick is just a bunch of red dust. It's an inferior brick, because it fell apart while I was holding it. Here you take it back."

Looking at Scooter with a scared look in his face, Jake replied, "It's true what I heard about you. You're tougher than you look. I was told that you're also a nutcase, because you always seem to have your head in the clouds. Don't hurt me. You can have the match. I'm getting out of here."

Jake then turned and climbed out of the ring and ran to his dressing room.

The referee again raised Scooters arm and declared him the winner by default. Scooter then walked back to his corner.

"Well see, you didn't have a thing to worry about," reasoned Hannibal. "You though you was afraid of Jake and instead he was afraid of you. You didn't have to lay a hand on him."

"That should make Charlie's silent partner happy this time," added Stephen. "You didn't even get a chance to sing and dance."

"Oh it was nothing. It was just in a day's work," replied Scooter. "He wasn't so tough and on top of that, he's not a very good judge of bricks."

The next morning the headline, of the sports section of the local newspaper read;

"Scooter, The Brick Victorious Over Jake, The Jack Hammer"

"Last night at Jerry Dickerson's Gym on Elmore Avenue in Davenport, Scooter, The Brick won his second wrestling match without laying a hand on his opponent, Jake, The Jack Hammer. Scooter, The Brick is becoming widely successful and a bigger sensation with each match.

Scooter entered the ring with his signature red plastic brick. Jake, The Jack Hammer revealed what was suppose to be a real brick he was hiding behind his back. Scooter, The Brick grabbed Jake, The Jack Hammer's brick out of his hand and crushed it with one hand. Jake, The Jack Hammer immediately left the ring in fear from Scooter's Strength.

Rumor has it that Scooter, The Brick makes what he calls vitamins from his chemicals. After he drinks these chemicals, it makes him super strong or does it. Could this just be a publicity stunt?

Time will tell as Scooter, The Brick will face Barney, The Buzz Saw at The Jerry Dickerson Gym next Saturday at 7: p. m. as the main attraction."

Chapter Twenty Three

WRESTLING WITH BARNEY, THE BUZZ SAW

A week passed and again Scooter was walking out of his dressing room at Jerry's Gym to meet with Barney, The Buzz Saw and walked into the ring. As Barney entered the ring he turned around and grabbed the top of the metal post in his corner with both hands and pulled on it, making the corner post taking the shape of a horse shoe. Scooter then walked up to the referee as before, facing Barney The Buzz Saw and began to shadow box.

Barney, The Buzz Saw was a foot taller than Scooter, The Brick and was packed full of muscle and looking the meanest of the other two wrestlers.

"Hey you. I just want to ask you a question. Don't ignore me. What's going on here? Tell me, just what do you think you are you doing? Are you looking for trouble?" asked Barney.

"I'm shadow boxing," replied Scooter.

"Just what do you know about shadow boxing?" asked a puzzled Barney.

"My friend Stephen taught me how to do it," answered Scooter. "Don't you think that's wonderful?"

"OK boys, come to the center of the ring so I can give you instructions," insisted the referee. "Listen, I want a good clean fight.

I don't want you pulling hair like this," said the referee as he pulled Scooter's hair. "I don't want you hitting with the fist like this or stepping on toes," the referee continued to say as he hit Scooter in the stomach and stepped on Scooter's toes.

Scooter then began to groan from the pain.

After the referee finished his instructions to the wrestlers, Scooter went on to say, "Barney, are you a tough guy?"

Barney just stood nose to nose with Scooter and didn't answer.

Scooter then asked Barney again, "Are you a tough guy?"

Still standing nose to nose with Scooter, Barney answered, "Yes I'm a tough guy."

"Oh, you're one of those tough guys. I just wanted to find out," answered Scooter.

"You don't look so tough to me," replied Barney. "My brother Stinky knows you. He went to high school with you and was always picking on you. You refused to fight back. I don't know how you frightened the other two wrestlers to make them run from you. I like it here and I'm not going to run. I don't like your looks. Your nothing but a pip squeak and as far as I'm concerned, your wrestling days are over. When I'm done with you, it will look like somebody walked over your grave because you and me are going to have a hoopty do."

"If you're going to wrestle me, next time be on time," instructed Scooter. "I'm not going to warn you again."

"What did you say?" asked Barney. "Are you talking to me? Are you talking to me?"

"Nothing I wanted you to hear. I was just talking to myself," answered Scooter.

"Mind your own business and don't talk so loud or I'm going to have to hurt you," answered Barney in a tough voice.

"I'm sorry if I said something to make you mad. Please don't hurt me," pleaded Scooter.

"OK, then just do what I tell you," instructed Barney. "I came here because I wanted to hear you sing and watch you dance."

"You really came here to hear me sing and to watch me dance?" answered a surprised Scooter.

"Yes, tough guy. Begin right now and it better be good," snarled Barney. "I want to hear the words nice and clear and then see you dance. Make it snappy."

"Stephen, Hannibal, Did you hear that? That was a nice gesture. He really does understand me and just wants to be nice to me. Barney likes me. He wants to hear me sing and watch me dance," shouted Scooter. "Barney, if I teach you the words and the steps, would you like to join me in doing The Brick? I think we should have a dance contest. Just wait a minute. I'll teach you how to do that."

"Scooter, put your hand out," instructed Barney.

Scooter then put his hand out.

"Now leave your hand out and put your foot out," demanded Barney.

Scooter then put his foot out along with his hand.

Barney then made a fist with his right hand and hit Scooter in the head, knocking Scooter on the mat. After Scooter stood up, he ran back to his corner, yelling for Stephen. Stephen immediately jumped over the ropes landing in the ring and walked up to Barney.

"Stop picking on my friend Scooter. He came here to wrestle you, not to box you," boomed Stephen. "Do you understand me?"

"I don't know who you think you are, but I guess you want some of this too," roared Barney as he took a swing at Stephen missing him.

"My name is Stunning Stephen Edwards and if you want to box, I will accommodate you," replied Stephen, while taking a jab at Barney, followed by a right cross, finished with a left hook overhand right combination, knocking Barney on the floor of the mat. "Just for your information, I am The World Middle Weight Boxing Champion," Stephen went on to say. "You don't seem very interested in wrestling Scooter, The Brick."

"And what if I don't want to wrestle Scooter, The Brick?" answered Barney.

"You'll do it alright. You can get out of this wrestling match the hard way by boxing me or you can wrestle Scooter, The Brick. Now do you want to box me or wrestle my friend Scooter? I'm sure you don't want to box me. Which will it be? You have all the time you need to think it over like ten seconds."

"I'm sorry. I didn't know it was you," answered Barney.

"Let me take a crack at him," offered an angry Ace. "I would like to soften him up, so he isn't so mean, before he wrestles Scooter."

"That's not necessary. I will wrestle Scooter without getting mean about it," insisted Barney.

"I didn't think so," replied Stephen.

"Then stop wasting time. Get up on your feet and get ready to wrestle," instructed the referee.

"OK Scooter, duty calls. What are you waiting for? It's time to get out there and do your duty by wrestling Barney. I want you to fight like a bull fighter. While your at it, be like a matador and enjoy yourself," demanded Hannibal. "Take care of this guy. Start wrestling and show him he isn't going to get off so easy. This is another match you're going to win."

"Alright, I'll wrestle Barney. Where's my brick?" asked Scooter.

"It's in your hand. Quite stalling and get out there and wrestle," scolded Hannibal.

"Don't rush me. I'm going. I'll take care of it," replied a reluctant Scooter. "After this, don't get me mixed up with any more of your schemes."

As Scooter entered the center of the ring, Barney asked, "What's the problem?"

"Are you ready for me to start singing and dancing?" asked Scooter.

"No, let me put you in a hold," replied Barney.

"Are you sure? I do have some tricks up my sleeve, along with a box of raisins to eat while I'm waiting to explain to you how this is done, so lend me your ears, asked Scooter.

Barney then put his right arm around Scooter's head and then grabbed both of Scooter's ears, pulling on them and asked, "How about these ears?"

"Not those ears. Those are my ears," screamed Scooter. "When I said lend me your ears, I meant for you to listen to me how we should get started. I thought I was suppose to start off singing and dancing,"

"You old dried up sack of bones. If you knew how to start, why did you ask me? Talking to you is like trying to open up a door and having the door knob come off." asked Barney as he grab-ed Scooter by the neck, putting him into a head lock. "I've wasted enough time with you."

"I wasn't sure which was the right way to start, but I was certain you would pick the wrong way to start. Your suppose to follow me. This isn't how it's suppose to go," explained an angry Scooter as he pulled Barney's arm away from his head without any trouble.

"I'm suppose to drop my plastic brick on your foot and then do my dance called the brick and sing. After that, I'm suppose to chase you all over the ring. Don't you know anything?"

"Stop biting your fingers!" yelled Barney's manager to Barney," "Do you want to get blood poisoning?"

Scooter then dropped his brick on Barney's foot and began to dance and sing. With a puzzled look on his face, Barney became perturbed by Scooter's increasing control of the match and exclaimed,

"Just what are you trying to do to me?"asked Barney. "Just what are all of you trying to do to me? Your nuts. You're all nuts and I think Scooter, The Brick is not on the level. I hate matches with stupid wrestlers and I'm going to leave."

"I know stupid wrestlers can be like animals," answered Scooter.

"They can be like mad dogs," replied Barney.

"You forgot to mention pigs," added Scooter. "Just who are we talking about anyway?"

"Who do you think we're talking about?" laughed Barney. "Scooter, The Brick."

"I think I got into the wrong conversation," cried Scooter.

"Anybody that would talk me into having a wrestling match with Scooter, The Brick is hopelessly brainless. He's not so smart, this guy. Stupid is as stupid does. In fact I think Scooter is seriously mentally ill or maybe he has a brain freeze.

I think there is a complex question about how it would be better for Scooter to keep his brains out of the way so he can keep an empty mind by not thinking. The simple answer to do that is he should take a nice walk to open up his brain and clear his mind of the stupid things he says when he opens up his mouth. Then excellence might just happen when he wrestles. Ha ha. Hee hee. Stranger things have happened."

"That's not a very nice thing to say to me. Give me back my brick," boomed Scooter. "I never wanted to wrestle to start with because I thought I was going to get hurt. You are the third professional wrestler that faced me that looked tough and acted tough. Instead I won the match without even laying a hand on you or the other two wrestlers.

You are all pussy cats, fraidy cats. Your probably afraid of your own shadow. You may call me crazy. All I have to do is read a book and I will still smarter than you. When I went to school, I was so smart my teacher was in my class for six years. I think the wages of stupidity is to hunt for another job. Instead of wrestling, maybe you should all work as baby sitters."

This made Barney really mad and he then began to make another fist to hit Scooter.

"Don't even think about it," yelled Stephen. "Either wrestle Scooter or get out of the ring."

Barney then turned around and walked over to his manager in his corner of the ring. "Forgive me if we don't shake hands," said an angry Barney to his manager. Barney then started slapping the manager's left check and then his right check, back and fourth.

When Barney was through slapping his manager, Barney started to climb out of the ring and he shouted at his manager, "Do you realize that you signed me up to wrestle the most stubborn, self deluded, bull headed wrestler I ever had to deal with? You wrestle Scooter, The Brick. I'm getting out of here before he has me talking to myself."

"What an ugly thing to say" replied Barney's manager. "Does that mean we're not friends anymore?"

"Hey Barney, I forgot you was still here. Run along. Go ahead and get out of the ring. If you change your mind, the wrestling is over here," laughed Scooter as Barney continued to climb out of the ring and started to walked back to his dressing room when a woman in the audience stood up in front of Barney.

"I work a full time job," said the woman. "Would you be interested in baby sitting my two kids?"

With a discussed look on his face, Barney didn't answer the woman and continued to walk back to his dressing room. The referee then called Scooter over to the center of the ring. He raised Scooter's right arm, declaring him the winner.

"That a boy," yelled Hannibal. "Well Scooter, it looks like you've won again. I can't give you enough credit. That's the first thing that you've done right."

Chapter Twenty Four
THE SILENT PARTNER

The next morning, the entire gang is now eating breakfast at Columbo's house. As they were eating, Columbo began to read the local newspaper to every body.

"Listen everybody. The headlines has now reached the front page about Scooter's third wrestling match," announced Columbo. "Listen to this."

"Scooter, The Brick Wins His Third Wrestling Match"

"Last night at Jerry Dickerson's Gym here in Davenport, Scooter, The Brick defeats Barney, The Buzz Saw without laying a hand on him. Barney, The Buzz Saw accused Scooter, The Brick of being mentally ill and declined to wrestle Scooter, The Brick.

Scooter replied, "You look tough and you act tough. You're just a pussy cat like the other two men that faced me to wrestle. Maybe the three of you should get jobs as baby sitters."

The question is Scooter, The Brick really mentally ill or is he using brains over brawn?

Will Barney, The Buzz Saw, Jake, The Jack Hammer and Barry, The Bone Crusher get jobs as baby sitters?

Time will tell. At this time, Scooter, The Brick doesn't have any more matches in his future.

If there are any wrestlers willing to face Scooter, The Brick, they are to contact Jerry Dickerson. If they are afraid to face Scooter, The Brick, Jerry will find them jobs as baby sitters."

"Since I was working with Scooter after the match, I haven't heard, did you locate anybody in the audience who might be Jerry's silent partner?" asked Stephen.

"With Scooter's success as a non wrestler, you might say, there was a huge audience there last night," replied Columbo. "Rex and me saw Dr. Nejino at the match. We asked him if he was a wrestling fan or what other reason he had for coming to the match. He told us that since Dr. Zodiac appeared through his lips at Margret's treatment, that he had to come and see Scooter's act."

"Did he like Scooters singing and dancing?" asked Stephen.

"It appeared that he was hiding something and he didn't really say," answered Columbo.

"Charlie came back to Davenport a couple of days ago," added Rex. "I was planning to call him this morning to see if he has heard from his silent partner."

"Since we're all here, why don't you call Charlie now?" quizzed Stephen.

"I'll do that right now," replied Rex. "Margret, have you seen my cell phone?"

"It's right on the coffee table where you left it," answered Margret. "I don't know how you can manage to be a Detective when you can't keep track of your own things. I'll go get it for you so you don't get lost on the way."

"Very funny, Margret. Very funny," laughed Rex. "You must be feeling better. Now you're starting to sound like Scooter."

"Who is this man, Scooter you keep talking about?" asked Margret.

"Over here mam," replied Scooter as he raised his hand. "Remember, I was going to make you some French Scrambled Eggs."

"So your the crazy wrestler everybody keeps talking about," observed Margret as she handed Rex his cell phone. "I don't know why the other wrestlers are afraid of you. You don't look so tough. In fact, you seem like a nice young man."

"Margret, just sit down and eat your breakfast," insisted Rex as he punched in the numbers of his cell phone to call Charlie and then he hung up right away.

"What am I doing? I can't call Charlie and ask him about his silent partner," Rex went on to say as everybody laughed. "I'm not even suppose to know about his silent partner. Jerry, I think you better call him."

"Rex, just sit there and eat your breakfast and let Jerry call this Charlie, whoever he is," replied Margret as everybody continued to laugh.

Jerry then looked around for his cell phone and couldn't find it.

"Now what did I do with my cell phone?" asked a confused Jerry.

"It fell on the floor and landed right under your chair," laughed Dixie as she picked it up and handed it to Jerry.

"You know, sitting here eating breakfast with all of you makes everybody feel like family to me," insisted Jerry as he punched in Charlie's number on his cell phone.

"Hello Charlie. This is Jerry calling. Now that Scooter has had three matches, have you heard from your silent partner?"

"You bet I have," answered Charlie in a very nervous voice. "He isn't very happy one bit. He was at Scooter's match last night and saw Scooter doing his singing and dancing. He said Scooter is making Dr. Zodiac a laughing stock by his actions. He insists that I fire Scooter or he will eliminate Scooter from wrestling, permanently.

He wants me and my other partners to go after the managers of the three wrestlers who faced that dreaded Scooter and sign their wrestler's contract's over to replace Scooter. If I don't get the wrestler's contracts within a week, he will eliminate me. After he hung up, I went to my medicine cabinet to get that bottle of pain pills, marked Scooter."

"You have nothing to worry about. Me and my partners will have those contracts before you can say, Jack Sprat. I should be getting back to you with all of those contracts in a couple of days," replied Jerry. "And as of now I will inform Scooter that he's fired."

"You don't have much time. Get those contracts signed over as soon as possible," pleaded Charlie.

"I'm on it. Just in case for some reason we can't find all three managers, I think you better leave Davenport until I contact you," suggested Jerry. "Don't forget to take those pain pills marked Scooter with you."

"You don't have to tell me twice. I don't know what to expect from my silent partner. My bags are already packed and I'm leaving on a jet plane for the Twilight Zone right now," insisted Charlie. "I better go. Call me when it's safe to come back to Davenport. Good by."

"What did Charlie have to say?" asked Columbo.

"I have some good news and some bad news," answered Jerry. "The good news is that Scooter did his job very well with his singing and dancing. It struck a nerve with Charlie's silent partner and Scooter doesn't have to wrestle anymore. I guess there is really no bad news, because our plan worked and we can move forward to the next phase."

"Ah gee. I was just starting to have fun with these wrestling matches," objected Scooter. "I didn't get hurt like I thought I was going to and I want to wrestle some more."

"Sure you've been in three wrestling matches and you faced three tough wrestlers. You bluffed them enough that they was more afraid of you than you was of them," insisted Hannibal. "You just don't know how lucky you've been. I think you better quite before you face a wrestler that will wrestle you and then you will get hurt."

"Says who?" asked Scooter.

"Says me," answered Hannibal as he reached over to try and hit Scooter. "If you want to wrestle so bad, lets go out in the back yard and you can wrestle me."

"Ooh, ooh, ooh, oh no never mind you don't. I'm an honorary Police Detective. You can't wrestle me, because Uncle Columbo says your my assistant," replied Scooter. "Uncle Columbo, tell Hannibal he can't wrestle me."

"What are you afraid of?" asked Uncle Columbo. "You already faced three very mean wrestlers and won the three matches. Because you're undefeated, I'm not going to help you."

"But those weren't really wrestling matches. Those guys was afraid to wrestle me. It's a good thing they didn't wrestle me. I might have gotten hurt. Hannibal isn't afraid of me and if I wrestle him, I will get hurt!" yelled Scooter. "Ulp, help, Stephen! Nobody will help me. I'm in trouble again! Where's my vitamins? Where's my brick?"

"I'm sorry. I can't help you," laughed Stephen. "I'm afraid your on your own."

"OK Scooter, that's quite enough. Hannibal isn't going to wrestle you," laughed Rex. "I want to hear the rest of what Charlie told Jerry."

"As I was saying," Jerry continued to say, "Charlie's silent partner says Scooter's singing and dancing is making a laughing stock out of Dr. Zodiac and because of that, he wants Charlie to fire Scooter from wrestling or he will eliminate Scooter for keeps.

Next he wants Charlie and his partners, which is us, to go after the managers of Barney, The Buzz Saw, Jake, The Jack Hammer and Barry, The Bone Crusher's managers, to get them to sign over their contracts to us. He is giving Charlie a week to get this done. I suggested to Charlie to leave town again."

"As police officers, we can't force the wrestler's managers to sign their boys over to us," noted Rex. "Jerry, you better call Charlie before he leaves town. Find out how he contacts his silent partner. You, Ace and the rest of your boys better get those contracts. Tell the managers that they will still manage their wrestlers. Only they are to work out in your gym and report to you.

Then call Charlie's silent partner and tell him that after Charlie talked to him, he decided to leave Davenport for good. Now he has to deal with you and your boys."

A couple of minutes later, Jerry hung up from Charlie after getting the phone number to to his silent partner.

"I got the number to Charlie's silent partner," addressed Jerry to the group. "I'm dialing his number right now. Hello, this is Jerry Dickerson. I am one of Charlie, The Chill's partners. Who do I have the pleasure of speaking with?"

"You know that I'm not going to tell you what I don't want you to know," answered a familiar voice on the phone. "Where is Charlie? He's the only one that I deal with."

"Not anymore," replied Jerry. "Charlie left town. Scooter, The Brick has retired from wrestling. Me and my partners are going to make the three wrestling managers sign their boys over to us, to replace Scooter, The Brick. Since I own a gym on Elmore Avenue, these managers can bring their boys to my gym to train where I can keep an eye on them.

Now you have to deal with me. Whatever kind of deal you had with Charlie isn't going to be enough. As a silent partner you have been getting most of the gravy. There are more of us and we are using my gym, so we need a larger percentage of the dough for what we can do. We will be taking most of the risks."

"Charlie wasn't doing the job I wanted with these managers," answered the silent partner. "Since you own a gym, and your experienced in these matters, it looks like it's going to be better that I deal with you."

"What have you got to contribute as a partner?" asked Jerry.

"I've got ways to find out things about managers, who makes big money with their wrestlers and then make them targets to deal with," answered the silent partner.

"What do you mean targets to deal with?" asked Jerry.

"I'm not going to explain everything to you. That's why I know who Charlie is and he doesn't know who I am. I know who all of you are, but you're not going to find out who I am. Take it or leave it?" replied the silent partner.

"I guess we'll try it your way for a while to see how it goes," proposed Jerry. "We need to know who you are. We're all in this to make some serious money. If I see you're not carrying your weight, we'll move on with out you. Do you understand me?"

"You're not going to find out who I am. If you did, I wouldn't like that at all. I'm not going to compete with you because I want it all," reasoned the silent partner. "Don't even think of trying it or I will have to eliminate you. Do we have an understanding? Do you understand me?"

"I understand and I don't like this arrangement," objected Jerry. "We all want the money and we'll do as you say for now."

"Then go after these managers today and get their boys to sign with you," ordered the silent partner.

"Now wait a minute. I'm not going to take any orders from you or anybody else," roared Jerry. "You may have scared Charlie so he would do as he was told. We may be partners, but as you told me, I have the experience, so I'm going to do things my way."

"OK, OK, I get the message. Now that we understand each other, I'll leave it to you to get the job done," promised the silent partner. "I want to make some serious money just like you. Keep me informed about the managers and the wrestlers. If I have anymore leads or ideas, I'll get back to you."

"I tried, but I couldn't find out who he was," said Jerry as he hung up. "His voice sounded familiar, but I couldn't quite place it. It sounded to me like it was Dr. Nejino. He insists that we go get the contracts from the managers of the three wrestlers that faced Scooter. What do we do now?"

"I think we should contact the managers and have them all meet at your gym," suggested Stephen. "Instead of getting the contracts for keeps, we need to have them meet with you, Rex, Columbo and myself to explain to them what's going on. We need to have them sign over the contracts to us with the understanding that they will get them back as soon as this case is solved."

"I agree with Stephen," replied Columbo. "What do you think Rex?"

"I think it's a good idea, only we don't tell the managers anymore than they need to know," answered Rex.

"Jerry, how sure are you that voice on the phone could possibly be Dr. Nejino?" asked Stephen.

"The more I think about it, I would say it is very likely that it is him," answered Jerry.

"Then I have a plan for our next move," explained Stephen. "I think we should make an appointment with Dr. Nejino to have him give a treatment to Scooter, because Scooter is taking it very hard in his part of the death of Dr. Zodiac. Along with Scooter, I think Charlie, Jerry, Hannibal and myself should be at this treatment. If he is really surprised to see Charlie at the treatment, that should prove he is Charlie's silent partner."

"It sounds to me that things are starting to add up," replied Rex. "Columbo and me saw and talked to Dr. Nejino at Scooter's wrestling match. He said he was there to watch Scooter perform his musical act about Dr. Zodiac. I wonder if Dr. Nejino and Dr. Zodiac are the same person. Go ahead and make that appointment for poor ole Scooter."

"No, no, and no. You're not getting me involved in any more of your schemes!" yelled Scooter as he got up to leave the room.

"Scooter, come back here and sit down," yelled Hannibal. "Now sit there and listen to Uncle Columbo."

"Uncle Columbo, You always think you can talk me into doing anything you want me to do! You can't make me!" objected Scooter. "I'm not going to do it! I won't do it!"

"Are you sure? Are you really sure?" asked Uncle Columbo. "As an Honorary Police Detective, you did a good job by following orders as a wrestler, beyond and above the call of duty. Because of that, I was going to promote you to Honorary Detective Sergeant because you have been chosen to lead a top secret assignment. It's an assignment that involves the highest security. I guess you don't want the promotion. Since you won't accept your next assignment, I can't promote you to Detective Sergeant Scooter."

"Says who?" replied Scooter.

"Says me," answered Uncle Columbo.

"If I do this, will Hannibal still be my assistant and he will have to do everything I tell him?" asked Scooter.

"He will have to follow your orders, the same way you will have to follow mine, Sergeant Scooter," answered Uncle Columbo.

"Did you hear that Hannibal? Now that I'm a Sergeant and you're still my assistant, I order you to make an appointment with Dr. Nejino," ordered Sergeant Scooter. "I'm feeling just awful for what I did to Dr. Zodiac. I need him to give me a treatment as soon as possible. Hannibal, did you hear me?"

"Yes Sergeant Scooter," replied Hannibal as he saluted Sergeant Scooter. "Uncle Columbo, how soon should I make the appointment?"

"I'll answer that question," offered Stephen. "We need to call Charlie and make sure he doesn't leave Davenport. As soon as we know Charlie is going to be at the treatment, we can make the appointment. Scooter, remember, if Dr. Nejino asks you any questions, you know nothing."

"Oh, I can handle that," promised Scooter.

"I know," answered Uncle Columbo. "Perfect, Everything is going like clockwork."

"We must have, oh, I'll arrange that. I'm sure I can be of little help. I'll make the appointment. You can depend on me," reasoned Scooter.

"I will arrange it. Just leave it to me. I will make the appointment. I'd rather depend on me," reassured Uncle Columbo.

"Now that you mention it, so would I. Uncle Columbo, I just want to know one thing?" asked Scooter. "What is a treatment?"

"It's kind of hard to explain. It has something to do with spooks. Your not afraid of spooks are you?" replied Uncle Columbo.

"Spooks? Of course I'm afraid of spooks. Who isn't? Tell me, just what did I agree to do this time?" insisted Scooter.

"You mean to tell me that you just defeated three tough wrestlers with out laying a hand on them. We all thought you was as tough as nails and now you are telling all of us that your afraid of a few measly spooks," answered Uncle Columbo. "I bet these very tough wrestlers who was afraid to face you wouldn't do the job that I assigned to you Sergeant Scooter. We all know they would be afraid of spooks and wouldn't do the job.

When Dr. Nejino gives somebody a treatment, he uses spooks to get the job done. These spooks won't hurt you. Charlie, Jerry, Stephen and Hannibal will be sitting right there with you."

"I've had more than enough. I won't do it. I just won't," roared Scooter. "You always save the worst part until last. First you get me to box Ace. Then you get me to wrestle professional wrestlers. Now you want me to deal with spooks. Your always asking me to be in on your schemes. Since this is another one of your crazy schemes where I have to deal with spooks, count me out."

"Your right. I always turn to you for your help with these schemes and it always mystifies me," answered Columbo.

"Scooter, think about what you did to me," responded Rex. "You came into my chemistry class and made a bomb. Then you threw it out the window where it landed on my new car and blew it up. You switched your chemicals, with the chemicals I was going to drink. I drank your chemicals by mistake and it turned me into a forty inch small fry. I lost my job at the college and I turned to a life of crime."

"So I did some stupid things. I'm always doing stupid things," replied Scooter. "At least these were crazy ideas I came up with."

"Uncle Columbo, it doesn't sound like you have the right man for the job. This sounds like a fun job to me. If Scooter won't do this, I'll do it if you make me an Honorary Detective Sergeant and make Scooter my assistant," asked Hannibal.

"Oh no you don't Hannibal. Uncle Columbo asked me to do this first," insisted Scooter. "I'm going to be the sergeant and your going to be my assistant. Isn't that right Uncle Columbo? Your not going to let Hannibal take the job away from me, are you?"

"Why no Scooter. Hannibal wouldn't know how to do the job. Nonsense. By all means your the best man for the job. We can't do this job with out you. The job is yours," promised Uncle Columbo.

"I can do the job. I'm not afraid of the spooks. I can deal with the spooks," reasoned Scooter. "What am I saying? I think I missed my chance to keep my mouth shut. Uncle Columbo, you tricked me into taking the job. You can give the job to Hannibal," pleaded Scooter.

"Why Scooter, are you going to cooperate with me or are you going back on your word that you would do the job?" asked Uncle Columbo. "You're going to be perfectly safe. Nothing is going to happen to you. If it does, we will all come to your funeral."

"What a big comfort that is. If it does come to that, I'll never speak to you as long as I live," promised Scooter. "If it comes to that, I will come back as a spook and scare the daylights out of all of you."

Chapter Twenty Five
SCOOTER'S TREATMENT

It is now two days later at ten in the morning. A nervous Scooter is in Dr. Nejino's office waiting for Dr. Nejino to come in and give him, his treatment. Sitting next to Scooter is Hannibal, Stephen, Charlie and Jerry. Dixie enters the room followed by Dr. Nejino. Dr. Nejino then again lay-ed on the bed as he did before while Dixie blindfolds him and then tied his hands and feet together. She then turned all the lights out again, except for the small light behind the desk.

Again a white sheet and a ball bat hovered through the air behind Hannibal, Stephen, Charlie and Scooter. A hand landed on Scooter's right shoulder. Feeling something on his shoulder, Scooter turned around to see what it was. Scooter then began to nudge Hannibal in desperation and began to yell, "Ooh, ooh, ooh," as he pointed at the hand on his right shoulder. As Hannibal looked at the hand, it moved to Hannibal's left shoulder. Hannibal then nudged Stephen, and pointed at the hand, yelling for help as the hand left Hannibal's shoulder and disappeared.

"Calm down you two," instructed Stephen. "This is all just part of the act."

As before, Dixie began to say, "I want complete silence from everybody as we begin. There is great danger in what we are all about to see and hear. I must warn all of you that death is present. Dr.

Nejino's body can play no part as to what happens. The spirits will take over his body completely."

Dr. Nejino then bean to say, "A spirit is crying out. The unbelievers must know that a spirit is trying to get through and he will be speaking through my lips. It's Dr. Zodiac. Speak you unhappy spirit."

"Charlie, I have a message for you. You haven't been making me very happy lately. It's time for me to execute your demise here and now," promised Dr. Zodiac. "Scooter, The Brick, because of you, you created my demise. You won three wrestling matches with your brick and the vitamins you drink that makes you very strong. You are making fun of me with your singing and dancing. Now I really hate you. Make no mistake. It's revenge I'm after. Take my advice and love every second and live it right up to the hilt. My violence is going to appear and will put your power in jeopardy. Now I'm back and your next."

After Dr. Zodiac spoke, all the lights went out and now the room was dark. Charlie made a hideous yell and fell to the floor.

"Dixie, turn the lights on right now!" yelled Stephen.

After fumbling around in the dark room, Dixie finally found the switch to the lights and she turned them on. To everybody's surprise Charlie had disappeared.

"Now what happen to Charlie?" asked Jerry. "He's disappeared. This is getting to be very strange that it's scary. It looks like Dr. Zodiac is responsible for Charlie's disappearance.

Stephen, when you was a Police Detective, you was always trying to pin these murders on me. By what we have seen and heard, this should prove that Dr. Zodiac is responsible for these killings and Charlie's disappearance."

"I don't disagree with you one bit," answered Stephen. "Dr. Zodiac is dead so how could he even be in this room. It's impossible how he kills people. Charlie's disappearance is another question to be answered. It seems like Dr. Zodiac is either invisible or he's just not here.

There has to be some kind of trick to this. This is going to be a hard one to figure out. Because Charlie was our partner, I want to find Charlie and now. It looks like I am going to have to take some time to study on it. I know what I want and I'm going to get it. After I put all of the pieces together, then I will be able to solve this riddle and find Charlie and Dr. Zodiac."

"Nobody can do the things that Dr. Zodiac does. That's because he believes in the super natural," reasoned Dr. Nejino. "Charlie and the rest of you was warned at the beginning of this session that death was present."

"Nobody is to leave this room. It looks like I have to report this murder and call my UN-favorite Davenport Detectives, Rex and Columbo to investigate Charlie's murder," insisted Stephen.

Chapter Twenty Six
CLUES TO THE BLOW GUN KILLINGS

The next morning, the gang was eating breakfast at Columbo's. Margret went to the front door to get the morning paper. As she walked toward the kitchen, she grabbed Rex's cell phone off of the coffee table in the living room.

"Here's the newspaper Rex and your cell phone you keep losing," offered Margret.

"I see the headlines are about Charlie's disappearance and murder," observed Jerry.

"How bad do they make the police look in the newspaper this time?" asked Stephen. "Rex, would you read it out loud for all of us to hear?"

Again the story in the local newspaper, the next morning read;

"Charlie, The Chill Disappears At Spook Treatment"

"A man in the wrestling profession known as Charlie, The Chill disappeared in Dr. Nejino's office, yesterday. Charlie was in Dr. Nejino's office while Scooter, The Brick was getting a treatment with spooks for a mental condition, when all the lights went out and Charlie disappeared.

It is a mystery to those in attendance as to how Charlie disappeared. Those people setting next to Scooter, The Brick Hickenbottom as he was getting his treatment was Jerry Dickerson, Hannibal Columbo,

Charlie, The Chill and Stunning Stephen Edwards. Dixie Doneright was assisting Dr. Nejino.

Stunning Stephen Edwards is The World Middle Weight Boxing Champion and ex Davenport Police Detective, Hannibal Columbo and Scooter Hickenbottom run The West Side Kids Detective Agency here in Davenport. Jerry Dickerson owns a gym for boxing on Elmore Avenue. Charlie, The Chill manages wrestlers.

The only suspect for Charlie's disappearance is Dr. Zodiac who fell down an elevator shaft and died a few weeks ago. At Scooter's treatment, through Dr. Nejino's lips, Dr. Zodiac says he has returned and is planning the demise of the people who has challenged his beliefs of the super natural.

Since Halloween is only a few days away, could this be a publicity stunt to give every body in the Quad Cities a good Halloween scare? Because of what is unknown, the public is asked to stay indoors after dark and keep your doors and windows locked. In the mean time, trick or treating has been canceled in The Quad Cities until further notice.

If anybody has any information of Dr. Zodiac or these killings, you are asked to call the police. It seems the police needs all the help they can get to solve The Blow Gun Killings and that all of their clues disappeared like Charlie, The Chill. It may even turn out that these Detectives need a treatment with spooks by Dr. Nejino to clear their mind, so they can solve this case. It's kinda spooky, isn't it? Ha, ha, ha, BOO!"

"It doesn't look like the newspaper is being very kind to us," observed Columbo.

"I think I have an idea how Charlie and Dr. Fine was murdered while they were getting a treatment at Dr. Nejino's office," suggested Stephen. "It may take me a few days to figure this out completely. Now after thinking about it, I might have been slow to begin with, but now I'm sure I know that I've got it!"

"If your sure you have it, hang on to it so you don't loose it. I don't know what you're laying, but get up and we'll fry it for breakfast," exclaimed Scooter. "Come on. Tell us what did you learn?"

"Not to talk to criminals," replied Stephen. "I thought finding a hoodlum with a Zombie mask, a turbine and a white sheet over his body would be easy to find. I smell something wrong. You know, I've got a feeling this is going to be bigger than murder. I don't know, but I'm going to find out. I think Dr. Nejino has a double life of crime and murder and he thinks he's going to rule with an iron hand."

"And a head to match," added Hannibal.

"I think Dr. Nejino and Dr. Zodiac are one and the same person," Stephen went on to say. "Also, I think he's as crooked as a dog's hind leg. If we look a little deeper, we will find that he is also the silent partner. Understand now?"

"No," replied Jerry.

"Me neither," answered Hannibal.

"Good," laughed Stephen.

"I was beginning to think we had a tough case and there was a fat chance of finding the murderer. It may sound a little crazy, but what you said makes sense," replied Rex. "What can we do about it? Another case like this and I might join the FBI."

"It might get a little rough, but I've got a feeling I'm going to have to do this job myself and play patty cake with Dr. Nejino," replied Stephen.

"You can't do this alone," exclaimed Rex.

"Well I'm doing it," answered Stephen. "I want him to know I mean business and may have to show Dr. Nejino the best right cross he's ever seen. I'm going to follow the advice in the newspaper and make an appointment to get a treatment by Dr. Nejino."

"What are you trying to do, commit suicide? Are you sure you want to do that?" objected Rex. "Aren't you afraid of the job? There must be some other way. I wouldn't trust Dr. Nejino as far as I could throw a piano."

"Exactly," answered Stephen. "Dr. Nejino has to be exposed for who he is and it looks like I'm elected to do it. He's the worst criminal I've ever seen. I'm going to see that he gets what's coming to him, because he is doing way more harm than good to the people who live in The Quad Cities."

"That could be very dangerous. You could be the next one murdered," insisted Rex. "Don't let me spoil your fun."

"It may sound that way. But as the spider said to the fly, "Come join me on my web," explained Stephen. "Now that I'm sure I know who the killer is, I also have it figured out how he killed Dr. Fine. If I'm right, I will catch him in the act. I have no idea how Dr. Fine and Charlie disappeared from under our noses."

"I can't believe what I'm hearing," said a surprised Dixie. "Dr. Nejino hired me and I have worked with Dr. Nejino and his spooks for a couple of years. He was also known as Michael, The Magnificent and Dr. Fine's Manager with his book, "The Healthy Benefits Of Hypnotism. I know he didn't like me working with Dr. Fine. It doesn't make any sense why he would kill Dr. Fine. I thought we were a team. Besides, I though Dr. Zodiac died when he fell down the elevator shaft at the hotel. I thought Detective Murphy was also Dr. Zodiac. What your telling us is very creepy. How can Dr. Zodiac still be alive?"

"We all would like to know what's going on with this. I think there was two Dr. Zodiacs. Detective Murphy was working with Dr. Nejino as partners," explained Stephen. "Are you willing to go through this again to find out? Remember, if Dr. Nejino and Dr. Zodiac are the same person and if this is true, he's got to be mentally ill. He has to be stopped and I plan on stopping him. Dixie, because of what I think, if you decide to help your life could also be in danger.

Remember, Dr. Zodiac threatened you while you were in bed. In his letter, he threatened all of us. If my plan works, we will catch him and then we can all return back to our normal lives."

"I would like that very much. I can't let you do this alone," answered Dixie. "Yet, I like staying at the Columbo's and I don't want to leave. It's like I have an extended family and I love it."

"We'll then I'll tell you what I'll do if Janet agrees with me," offered Columbo. "All of you can come to our house and do this for a week once a year."

"I agree with my husband," reasoned Janet. "If you want, we will also invite all of you to special occasions like Thanksgiving and Christmas, because you are extended family to us."

"Dixie, Stephen, I'm not going to let you do this alone. I'll take my chances with the rest of you. I'm going to be your back up and I'm going with you," insisted Jerry. "I realize that it is going to be a rough one, but all we can do is try."

"Jerry is right. You're not going to leave me out. You may need plenty of back up. I'm also going. I'm in on this with all of you," demanded Hannibal. "Since I've known Stephen, he always stands up for what is right. By the way, just how was Charlie and Dr. Fine killed?"

"People always thought I was crazy for the stupid things I have done. I know I'm going to regret saying this," reasoned Scooter. "I'm very scared about what I'm going to say. Hannibal, Stephen and Dixie are my friends. Now Jerry is my friend and everybody is always there for me. I'm not going to stay out of this scrape any longer. Now I'm going to be there for them. I'm also going."

"Scooter, if you go, this time obey orders and stay put. Somebody has to keep an eye on you and as always, I'm elected," explained Stephen. "As I said before, It might get a little rough if this man is mentally ill, but I think you will be fine.

It's good to know I have friends I can count on. Now I know we'll catch that murdering rat. I'm going to have Dixie call Dr. Nejino and make my appointment first and then I'll tell everybody what we're going to do next."

Chapter Twenty Seven

THE RESCUE OF THE GERMAN SHEPARD

Late that night a mysterious figure was seen looking in the windows in Northwest Davenport. Again it was a man with a Zombie mask, wearing a turbine, with a white sheet over his body, known as Dr. Zodiac.

As it approached 11:00 p. m. Dr. Zodiac was looking in a bedroom window where a blond lady in her 30's was sleeping in her bed. The window to the bedroom was half open. Dr. Zodiac removed the screen and climbed through the window. He pulled out a large knife from his pocket and then walked over to the sleeping woman. Reaching down, he began to shake her and then said, "Wake up Dixie Doneright. This is Dr. Zodiac speaking to you. Remember me. I'm the mysterious Scorpio, a seething villain, who is here to settle my score with you."

The woman then began to open her eyes and saw a man with a Zombie mask, wearing a turbine and a sheet over his body.

The man began to raise his right hand with a knife in it. The woman let out a curdling scream and then yelled for her husband, Jake for help. Hearing his wife scream, Jake with his German Shepard, rushed through the back door of the house to the bedroom. Seeing Dr. Zodiac standing there with his knife, Jake said to his German Shepard, "Go get him Mike!"

As the dog began running toward him barking, Dr. Zodiac started running in terror towards the window he came in. The German Shepard took a bite out of the left leg of Dr. Zodiac's pants and wouldn't let go. Dr. Zodiac then took of his pants with the dog still holding on to his pants with his teeth. Dr. Zodiac then jumped through the window, landing on his stomach. He quickly stood up and started running through the back yard and disappeared in the dark of the night.

The next morning in the local paper, the headlines read;

"German Shepard Takes a Bite Out Of Crime"

"It seems that Dr. Zodiac visited a woman in northwest Davenport last night while she was in her bed sleeping. A man wearing a Zombie mask, a turbine and a white sheet over his body nudged Donna Smithers on the should, waking her up and identified himself as Dr. Zodiac. As Donna's eyes began to open, she saw this hideous man standing over her with a knife in his hand.

Donna's husband, Jake Smithers came rushing through the back door of their house with his German Shepard, Mike to the rescue. Seeing this hideous man, Jake yelled to his dog, Mike to "Go get him". The German Shepard ran at Dr. Zodiac barking and grabbed his left pant leg. Dr. Zodiac slipped out of his pants, jumped out the bedroom window and escaped in the dark of the night.

The question is, how can Dr. Zodiac be roaming the city of Davenport when according to the police, he fell down the elevator shaft at a hotel in down town Davenport and died?

How can a dead person come back to life? How can people be murdered in front of the police and they don't know how it was done? Until the police get lucky and figure this out, secure your doors and windows for your safety. Start a neighborhood watch. If nothing else, get a German Shepard like Mike to watch over your family and house."

The following morning, the headlines in the local paper read;

"Dr. Zordiac Seen Again With Strange Accomplice"

"Last night it was reported to the police that two strange men was seen looking in windows in northwest Davenport last night. One of the men known as Dr. Zordiac was wearing a Zombie mask, a turbine and a white sheet over his body. The second man appeared to be half human and half ape.

No houses were broken into and nobody was hurt. Residents are urged not to confront these two men, because together they could be very dangerous. The public is asked to stay indoors after dark and keep your doors and windows locked.

If anybody has any information on these pair, they are to call The Police."

Chapter Twenty Eight
WHERE DID HE GO

It was finally two days later. It was 10:00 a. m. and Stephen, Jerry, Dixie, Hannibal and Scooter was sitting in Dr. Nejino's office.

"If you men would wait here, I'm going into the other room to prepare for Stephen's treatment," insisted Dixie.

"Can I come with you to help?" asked Scooter.

"Sure you can Scooter. I would appreciate your help," answered Dixie.

Ten minutes later after the two disappeared into the next room Hannibal said, "This place gives me the creeps. I think it was a mistake to let Scooter go with Dixie."

"I think your right. I was thinking about how I was going to handle the treatment and forgot about Scooter," replied Stephen. "We need to all stay together. Let's go find Scooter right now."

Dixie then appeared at the doorway to the next room and said, "You can't come in yet until the doctor is ready to see you."

"Where is Scooter?" demanded Stephen

"He was standing right behind me," replied Dixie.

"Scooter, come out of that room and now," ordered Stephen as he pushed his way past Dixie.

"Scooter isn't here. He's disappeared just like Charlie, The Chill" insisted Stephen.

"My best friend has disappeared! He's gone!" yelled Hannibal. "He can't be! Other than this door, there is no other way, in or out!"

"Dixie, what do you know about Scooter's disappearance?" questioned Stephen.

"There's nothing for Dixie to know," objected Dr. Nejino. "Like you said, the only way in or out of this room is through that doorway. The only logical answer is that the spooks kidnapped your friend."

"You call that logic? There's no such thing as spooks and you know it," insisted Hannibal as he grabbed Dr. Nejino by the collar of his shirt. "You've done something to Scooter. You've got him. If you hurt him in any way, I'm going to beat you so hard you spook chaser, that all the spooks in your body will vacate the premises."

"Hannibal, let Dr. Nejino go," demanded Stephen. "He isn't going to tell you anything.

Dr. Nejino, you sit in the chair by your desk while Hannibal keeps an eye on you. There has got to be another way out of here. Jerry, would you help me by pounding on these walls to see if there is a hidden exit in one of them?"

Jerry then began to pound on the wall behind Dr. Nejino's desk, hearing a hollow sound. A few moments later, Jerry yelled, "Stephen, I think I've got something here!"

Stephen then walked over behind Dr. Nejino's desk where Jerry was standing. Jerry then preceded in pounding on the wall again for Stephen to hear the hollow sound.

"There's got to be some kind of door in the wall," observed Stephen. "Look around for some kind of switch or button that will open up the door."

"I'm looking, but I can't find anything," insisted Jerry.

"I'm going to try the desk," answered Stephen as he turned around and sat down in the chair by the desk.

After searching a couple minutes for a button, Stephen felt a button inside the top drawer of the desk. Stephen hit the button and a door in the wall began to open.

"You found it, a secret room," exclaimed an excited Jerry. "Let's you and me go check it out."

"Hannibal, you keep an eye on this creep. He can be very tricky. Jerry and I are going into this next room to look for Scooter," instructed Stephen. "Come on Jerry. Stay close to me. I don't know what to expect. I don't have a gun or a flashlight, do you?"

"Of course I don't have a gun. I just got out of prison six weeks ago and I'm not allowed to carry one," explained Jerry. "If I did have a gun on me and got caught by the police with it, they would send me back to prison."

"I found a flashlight in one of the desk drawers. Now we can go in the other room. Just be careful," instructed Stephen.

After Stephen and Jerry entered the next room, Stephen shined the light on another door. Stephen opened up the door and exclaimed to Jerry, "Look, this is going to the basement. It's lucky for us that there is a switch at the top of the steps to turn the basement lights on."

After Stephen and Jerry went into the basement, they saw eight cages that looked like jail cells. In five of the cages was Scooter, Dixie, Charlie, Dr. Fine and a hairy half man, half ape. Over by the wall on the other side of the basement room stood a man, with a gun in front of two beds and some medical equipment.

"Look out, he's got a gun!" shouted Jerry.

"Who do we have here? What are you two doing here?" asked the man with the gun. "It doesn't matter, because I'm glad to have you with us because I've got two empty cages to put both of you in. I've got orders. Into the cooler you go. After your locked in, you will have no way to escape."

"The only orders I'm interested in are my own orders," objected Stephen. "Don't we get a trial or anything?"

"Nein," answered the man with a German accent.

"Your quit wrong. It must be 10:30 by now," insisted Stephen.

"I'm afraid I cannot accommodate you. This is Dr. Nejino's orders. Now get in the cells," replied the man with the gun. "I do appreciate your sense of humor. All of you will remain here permanently as Dr. Nejino's prisoners."

"Is there any way we can make a deal with you to release the prisoners you have and also let Jerry and me go?" asked Stephen.

"I will release you prisoners over my dead body," answered the man with the gun.

"That's the deal I'm looking for," laughed Stephen.

"As for you Scooter, I have some good news and some bad news for you," said the man with the gun. "The good news is that you have the kind of brain I have been looking for. The bad news is that my hairy friend over here needs a brain, so I'm giving him yours."

When the man was done talking, Stephen immediately threw his flash light at the man, knocking the gun out of his hand. Then he ran up to the man and hit him in the face with a right knocking the man to the floor. Jerry ran over to where the gun fell on the floor and picked it up and gave it to Stephen. Stephen then pointed the gun at the man and told him to sit quietly on the bed behind him.

"Well, well, well, what a pleasant surprise. Jerry, Stephen, I'm so glad to see you," cried Dixie who was sitting in her cage.

"Dixie, how did you get down here? I thought we left you upstairs," asked Jerry.

"That was my twin sister, Dorthy you left upstairs," explained Dixie. "Dr. Nejino brought Scooter and me down here a half hour ago and put us in these cages."

"Dixie, did I hear you right?" asked Stephen. "Jerry, You better go warn Hannibal right away about Dixie's twin sister before it's too late."

"I'm glad to have found all of you in one piece," said a surprised Stephen. "Dr. Fine, Charlie, I thought you died from a poison dart that was shot in the back of your neck."

"Those chemicals in the darts had a short effect on us. The chemicals made it look like we were dead," explained Dr. Fine. "Dr. Nejino was Charlie's silent partner. Dr. Nejino, also known as Michael, The Magnificent was the manager of my book, "The Healthy Benefits Of Hypnotism". He was afraid Charlie and I would expose him for who he really is. That's why he made it look like we were murdered and then dragged us down to these cages."

"Scooter, I'm glad your alright. Hannibal is very worried about you," insisted Stephen. "What's the story of this half man, half ape in this next cage?"

"You might say that Dr. Nejino created him like a Frankenstein," answered Dr. Fine. "Dr. Nejino was going to use him in our demise. You see those two beds over by that wall, with all of that medical equipment? Dr. Nejino was going to place Scooter on one of those beds and tie him down with leather straps. He was then going to put this creature on the other bed and fasten the leather straps on him.

That man sitting on the bed is Dr. Miles. He is the doctor who is known to give criminals new faces to escape the law. Dr. Miles was another partner of Dr. Nejino's. Dr. Miles was going to use that medical equipment to switch Scooter's brain to this creature and this creature's brain to Scooter."

"It's a good thing the creature didn't have his brain switched to Scooter's brain," responded Charlie. "The creature would have gotten the short end of the trade."

"How would you like that Scooter? You wouldn't need your vitamins or brick to wrestle. You would then be a big hairy wrestler with the muscles you need to wrestle without getting hurt," laughed Stephen.

"You and Charlie are not funny," replied Scooter as the creature let out a loud roar.

Scooter then turned to the creature and said, "Shut up and mind your own business!"

Hearing this, the creature looked at Scooter with a sad look on his face and then went to the back of his cage where he lay ed down.

"Scooter, take it easy. That's enough. It looks like you hurt his feelings by what you said," replied Stephen.

"I don't care. Just let me outa here. I don't know why I ever came to this place! I just want to go home!" answered Scooter as Jerry came running down the stairs to the basement.

Chapter Twenty Nine
Dr. Nejino has Escaped

"We've got troubles," yelled Jerry. "Dorthy hit Hannibal on the back of the head and knocked him out. Dr. Nejino and Dorthy has escaped."

"I know where Dr. Nejino is going," reasoned Dr. Fine. "He has gone to my office to get money and his personal papers about him out of my safe."

"Jerry, take this gun and point it at Dr. Miles while he gets the keys to let everybody out of their cages." replied Stephen. "After everybody is out of their cages, put Dr. Miles in the cage next to his hairy friend and lock the door, nice and tight. I'm going after Dr. Nejino."

Stephen then ran up the steps into the dark room, through the office and out to the drive way where his shiny new red sports car was parked. He jumped into his car, started the engine and drove away to Dr. Fine's office. As luck would have it, there was an empty parking spot in front of Dr. Fine's office.

Seeing Stephen's red sport car outside, Dr. Nejino picked up his brief case full of money and papers and ran out the back door of Dr. Fine's Office. After Stephen parked his car, he cautiously went into Dr. Fine's office and saw the door to the safe open.

"Dr. Nejino has been here," Stephen thought to himself. "He must have gone out the back door."

Following his instincts of being a professional boxer and Detective, Stephen also went out the back door of Dr. Fine's Office. Once outside, Stephen saw Dr. Nejino running towards Jerry's hotel. Stephen began to run after Dr. Nejino.

When Dr. Nejino approached the hotel, he ran around the back of the hotel where there was a fire escape. He jumped up and pulled the ladder to the fire escape down and began to climb up the fire escape. After reaching the third story, he looked down and saw Stephen at the bottom of the fire escape.

A window to an apartment was open right in front of him. Dr. Nejino climbed through the window into a living room, where an elderly couple was sitting watching a scary Halloween movie.

Seeing a small throw rug in front of the elderly couple, Dr. Nejino picked it up and through it out the window at Stephen.

"Hey what are you doing with my throw rug?" yelled the old woman as she stood up in front of Dr. Nejino.

"Get out of my way, old lady!" screamed Dr. Nejino as he pushed the woman back into her chair. Then he went over to the window, shut and locked it. Seeing Stephen still coming up the fire escape, Dr. Nejino ran out of the apartment into the hall way, looking for the stairs.

Within seconds, Stephen was standing outside the apartment of the elderly couple looking in the window. He began to knock on the window and said to the elderly couple

"I'm Detective Stephen Edwards. Would you be so kind as to let me in. I'm sorry to inconvenience you. I want to give you back your throw rug. As you can see, that man that went through your apartment is a violent criminal who mistreats throw rugs. He is involved in The Blow Gun Murderers and I need to catch him."

The woman then asked her husband if she should let him in.

The husband replied, "He seems like a nice young man. By all means, let him in."

The woman then unlocked the window and opened it and said, "I'm glad to have this window open again. It gets hot in here."

Stephen climbed through the window and handed the woman her throw rug and then ran out of the apartment into the hall way.

"Which one of the two men did you like the best?" asked the husband.

"I think I liked the second one the best. He was very polite. I would even like to ask him over to have a whiskey with us. The first one seemed very mean and scary," answered the woman. "He probably can't hold his liquor anyway."

"I also liked the second one the best," replied the husband. "I would never share my whiskey with the first one. He is not a very nice person."

Once in the hallway, Stephen went to the door where the steps was. He looked down the steps and didn't see Dr. Nejino. After listening for movement on the steps, he heard Dr. Nejino going up the steps. Stephen began to climb the steps at a fast pace, taking two steps at a time.

Once Stephen reached the roof of the hotel, he began to search for Dr. Nejino. Stephen then stopped by the door to the elevator shaft to his back. In a flash, Dr. Nejino jumped off of the roof of the elevator shaft on the back of Stephen, knocking him down to his knees. He hit Stephen in the head with his fist and then ran to the door to the elevator shaft.

Dr. Nejino opened the door and went inside and stood by a heavy duty iron fence surrounding. the elevator shaft and looked down the elevator shaft. His only chance of escaping was to go down the elevator shaft. A large heavy rag was setting on top of the metal fence by the gate. Dr. Nejino picked up the rag and wrapped it around the cables to the elevator. He jumped into the elevator shaft holding on to the elevator cables and began sliding down the cables.

Stephen stood up and looked around for Dr. Nejino and saw the open door to the elevator shaft. He ran into the elevator shaft by the metal fence and looked down the elevator shaft. Seeing Dr. Nejino sliding down the cables of the elevator he saw the elevator coming up the shaft with Dr. Nejino coming up with the elevator while he was still hanging on to the cables.

Dr. Nejino continued to slide down the cables and landed on the roof of the elevator. He opened the door to the roof of the elevator and jumped into the elevator.

Looking around, Stephen found another large heavy rag. He wrapped it around the elevator cables, jumped into the elevator shaft holding on to the cables and slid down to the elevator. When he reached the roof of the elevator, he jumped through the opening on the roof and jumped into the elevator facing Dr. Nejino as the elevator began to fall to the lobby of the hotel.

"They say dreams never come true. Your spooks aren't going to save you this time," promised Stephen. "Here we are. Just you and me and now your going to get a beating."

"Don't you even think of hitting me. I'm going to turn into a poisonous snake and I will bite you," insisted Dr. Nejino.

"You go ahead and do that," replied Stephen. "and while I'm waiting, take this, and have some sweet dreams."

Stephen then began to hit Dr. Nejino with his signature jab, followed by a right cross, finished with a left hook, with an overhand right combination as the elevator stopped and opened its doors at the hotel lobby. Down fell Dr. Nejino at Scooter's feet. Seeing Dr. Nejino at his feet, Scooter began to dance and sing, "Ouch, ouch. I'm Dr. Zodiac. I'm in pain. You lame brain. You idiot. Whoever walks around with a brick must be insane."

The next morning, everybody was sitting in Columbo's kitchen having breakfast. After bringing in the morning paper, Columbo read the headlines followed by the story;

"Stunning Stephen Edwards Solves Blow Gun Killings"

"Stunning Stephen Edwards has been credited to solving the Blow Gun Killings by the police. As a Police Detective, Stunning Stephen Edwards followed his instincts and with a hunch, developed the clues he needed to solve these Blow Gun Killings that has stumped the police department.

Dr. Nejino, with these other names of Dr. Zodiac and Michael, The Magnificent has mystified the police. Dr. Zodiac has been thought to have died by falling down an elevator shaft at a local hotel in east downtown Davenport. It is now known that Detective Murphy, Dr. Nejino's partner was playing the role of Dr. Zodiac at the time.

Detective Stunning Stephen Edwards made an appointment with Dr. Nejino to have a treatment with spooks. Jerry Dickerson, owner of a gym by the Davenport Casino, Hannibal Columbo, Scooter Hickenbottom and Dixie Doneright was in attendance for the treatment.

Before the treatment started, Scooter Hickenbottom, a wrestler also known as Scooter, The Brick and Dixie Doneright disappeared in Dr. Nejino's office. Detective Edwards and Jerry Dickerson searched Dr. Nejino's office for the pair. A hidden room was discovered behind a wall of the office leading down to the basement of Dr. Nejino's residence.

Dr. Miles, a partner of Dr. Nejino, who is known to give criminals new faces was found in the basement along with eight cages that resembled jails.

Dixie Doneright and Scooter Hickenbottom was found locked up in two of these cages. Charlie, The Chill and Dr. Preston Fine who was thought to be killed by poisonous darts was also found locked in these cages. A creature, half man, half ape was locked up in a fifth cage.

It was the intention of Dr. Nejino and Dr. Miles to switch Scooter Hickenbottom's brain into the creature.

Detective Stunning Stephen Edwards is also The World Middle Weight Boxing Champion. Stephen is planning to leave Davenport to go back to his profession of boxing.

Halloween is no longer canceled in the city of Davenport. The kids will now be allowed to trick or treat as their favorite spooks. The most favorite costume will be of Stunning Stephen Edwards, The World Middle Weight Boxing Champion followed by Dr. Zodiac and Scooter, The Brick"

Stunning Stephen Edwards leaves Davenport with Ace as his boxing manager.

Jerry Dickerson marries Dixie Doneright and becomes a Detective.

Jerry's crew manages his gym.

Hannibal, Scooter and the West Side Kids take over Dr. Nejino's business and treats people with spooks.

Margret becomes Scooter's best friend.

The hotel desk clerk gives tours of the Quad Cities.

Printed in the United States
by Baker & Taylor Publisher Services